The evening seemed like something in a play.

The perfect family holiday…before the aliens landed or the body was found or some other tragedy befell the players in the scene.

Sara gazed into the fire as a shiver rushed over her. Someone was walking over her grave, as her mother would once have said.

Hearing Cade's steps on the stairs, she carefully wiped all emotion from her face and waited, heart pounding. She wasn't sure what she was waiting for, but she knew, when her eyes met Cade's, that she'd lied to herself about her reasons for coming to his ranch.

It wasn't for fact-finding, but for herself and the hunger that refused to be suppressed any longer.

Dear Reader,

We're smack in the middle of summer, which can only mean long, lazy days at the beach. And do we have some fantastic books for you to bring along! We begin this month with a new continuity, only in Special Edition, called THE PARKS EMPIRE, a tale of secrets and lies, love and revenge. And Laurie Paige opens the series with *Romancing the Enemy*. A schoolteacher who wants to avenge herself against the man who ruined her family decides to move next door to the man's son. But things don't go exactly as planned, as she finds herself falling...for the enemy.

Stella Bagwell continues her MEN OF THE WEST miniseries with *Her Texas Ranger*, in which an officer who's come home to investigate a murder finds complications in the form of the girl he loved in high school. Victoria Pade begins her NORTHBRIDGE NUPTIALS miniseries, revolving around a town famed for its weddings, with *Babies in the Bargain*. When a woman hoping to reunite with her estranged sister finds instead her widowed husband and her children, she winds up playing nanny to the whole crew. Can wife and mother be far behind? THE KENDRICKS OF CAMELOT by Christine Flynn concludes with *Prodigal Prince Charming*, in which a wealthy playboy tries to help a struggling caterer with her business and becomes much more than just her business partner in the process. Brand-new author Mary J. Forbes debuts with *A Forever Family*, featuring a single doctor dad and the woman he hires to work for him. And the MEN OF THE CHEROKEE ROSE miniseries by Janis Reams Hudson continues with *The Other Brother*, in which a woman who always counted her handsome neighbor as one of her best friends suddenly finds herself looking at him in a new light.

Happy reading! And come back next month for six new fabulous books, all from Silhouette Special Edition.

Gail Chasan
Senior Editor

Please address questions and book requests to:
Silhouette Reader Service
U.S.: 3010 Walden Ave., P.O. Box 1325, Buffalo, NY 14269
Canadian: P.O. Box 609, Fort Erie, Ont. L2A 5X3

Romancing the Enemy

LAURIE PAIGE

SPECIAL EDITION®

Published by Silhouette Books

America's Publisher of Contemporary Romance

Special thanks and acknowledgment are given
to Laurie Paige for her contribution
to THE PARKS EMPIRE series.

To Judy, Allison and Vanessa
for the good times at Sundance.

SILHOUETTE BOOKS

ISBN 0-373-24621-8

ROMANCING THE ENEMY

Visit Silhouette Books at www.eHarlequin.com

Printed in U.S.A.

Books by Laurie Paige

LAURIE PAIGE

Laurie has been a NASA engineer, a past president of the Romance Writers of America, a mother and a grandmother. She was twice a Romance Writers of America RITA® Award finalist for Best Traditional Romance and has won awards from *Romantic Times* for Best Silhouette Special Edition and Best Silhouette in addition to appearing on the *USA TODAY* bestseller list. Recently resettled in Northern California, Laurie is looking forward to whatever experiences her next novel will send her on.

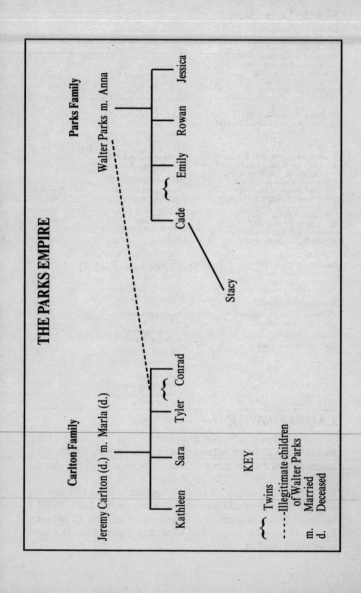

THE PARKS EMPIRE

Carlton Family

Jeremy Carlton (d.) m. Marla (d.)

Kathleen Sara Tyler Conrad

Parks Family

Walter Parks m. Anna

Cade Emily Rowan Jessica

Stacy

KEY

︷ Twins
----- Illegitimate children of Walter Parks
m. Married
d. Deceased

Chapter One

The private telephone line rang in the quietly luxurious office located above Parks Fine Jewelry, West-Coast rival to Tiffany's in New York.

Walter Parks lifted the receiver. "Yes?" he said without preamble. He listened to the message with no expression, then asked one question. "You're sure?"

The caller answered affirmatively.

"Send me a copy of the death certificate," Walter ordered the private detective. "No, not here," he said a trifle impatiently as if the man should have figured it out for himself. "To the post office box."

In twenty-five years, he'd well learned how to cover his tracks. The post office box was with a private postal service two doors down the street. No one in his family knew of it. But then, no one in the family knew much of anything that he didn't want them to know.

He replaced the phone and stood by the window, watching the December rain fall endlessly from the winter sky. The only place as cold and dismal as San Francisco could be in the winter was San Francisco in the summer on days when the coastal fog shrouded the city.

So. Marla was dead. About damned time. Twenty-five years he'd had to worry about her, and had even felt guilty at times about her and her pack of brats. But no more.

As his old man, poor as the proverbial church mouse, had often said—life was what it was and a man had to look after his own fate.

Walter had found that to be true. The gods of fortune smiled on those who grabbed each opportunity when it came along. A slow man was a loser. That man wasn't him.

Taking a deep breath, he tried to sense the weight rolling off his back, to experience the easing of it in his spirit. Realizing he didn't feel lighter in heart, body or soul, he grimaced. No matter. The last link to his past, the dangerous part of it at any rate, was gone.

He put a hand to his chest. A little heartburn there. He should eat healthier. He knew it. And no alcohol, except for a couple of glasses of wine. That was good for the ol' ticker, according to the doctors.

The rain pelted the windowpane in a wind-blown fury, sending an odd chill along the back of his neck. He rubbed the spot, then started as the phone rang again. Glancing at the light, he saw it was his office line.

"Parks," he said upon answering.

The caller was his oldest son, destined to one day run the company. Pride lifted his spirits. He and Anna had produced a fine brood, if he did say so himself.

Cade was the best of the bunch—smart, handsome and coolheaded. Walter had wanted the boy in the office with him, but Cade hadn't been interested in the diamond and jewelry business, the wheeling and dealing on a global level. He'd been fascinated by the law. Walter had conceded a lawyer wasn't a bad thing to have in the family.

Now the boy worked for a prestigious law firm— something Walter had personally seen to—and handled the business of the jewelry company from contracts to taxes. At twenty-nine, Cade already knew every aspect of the diamond trade. He was in position to take over when Walter needed him to. The boy's sense of responsibility would see to that.

"Cade, how about some lunch?" Walter asked in a jovial tone. "Top o'the Mark in half an hour?"

"Fine. I have the information you wanted on King Abbar and his son, Prince Lazhar, of Daniz. The king is ill. I understand the son handles most of the details of running the kingdom nowadays. Shall I bring the folder with me?"

"Yes."

Walter smiled as he hung up. Daniz was one of those tiny European countries most people had never heard of. Which showed how stupid most people were. Its diamonds were some of the finest in the world. A new find, its mines produced pink- and champagne-colored stones, which fortunately were becoming the rage among the celebrity crowd…with a few judicious gifts here and there on his part. A sharp deal with the ruler could be lucrative for them both.

Two pieces of good news in one day. A fine way to start the new year. The gods were truly smiling, even if the heavens were not. He instructed his secretary to call for his car and hardly noticed the rain as he headed to lunch.

Sara Carlton shivered as a gust of wind hit her. Someone needed to tell the weatherman that winter was six months ago and it was now June, not January.

Pulling her jacket closer around her, she stared at the elegant house standing shoulder-to-shoulder with a whole block of equally expensive Georgian-style homes.

Since she'd done her homework before moving from Denver to San Francisco, she knew a kindergarten teacher, which she was, couldn't afford the rent on such a prime piece of property in the St. Francis Woods area of the city. Fortunately she didn't have to.

"Isn't it lovely?" Rachel Hanson commented.

Rachel was a kindergarten teacher at Lakeside, a prestigious private school only three blocks from there and the place, come Monday, where Sara would also be employed. Rachel was also the older sister of Sara's best friend from her high-school days back in Denver. She had taken Sara under her wing when Sara had written for information about teaching positions in the city back in January.

Five years older than Sara's own twenty-nine years, Rachel had graduated from college, married and moved to the West Coast while the two younger girls had been high-school seniors. Her husband had abandoned her, so Sara assumed they were divorced. Rachel knew why Sara and her brother had returned to the area and was wholly sympathetic to their quest.

"Very much so," Sara agreed, her gaze sweeping over the tiny front yard and decorative wrought-iron fence that separated the patch of green from the street. "I can't believe my luck in getting to house-sit a mansion for six months. Are you sure your artist friend said it was okay?"

Rachel laughed at Sara's doubts. "You only get half the mansion," she corrected. "It's a duplex. And yes, I made sure we got permission in writing since the owner is actually a friend of a friend. Let's go inside."

The front walk widened to accommodate three steps and a marble-tiled stoop. Two identical doors—both white with leaded oval windows in beveled, frosted panes that formed a woodland scene on each—were set side-by-side in the sheltered alcove and gave entrance to the two homes.

Rachel had explained in a letter that the mansion was divided into two town houses, which meant the bedrooms of each were directly over their respective living room-kitchen-den areas, which afforded the maximum privacy for each occupying family.

Sara inserted the key Rachel had handed her and opened the door on the left. The chill of an unoccupied house rushed over her as she stepped into the foyer. It settled along her spine like the touch of a cold, unfriendly hand…a ghost who wasn't happy at her intrusion, she surmised.

"There's a fireplace," Rachel said. "This place could use some heat. Let's see if we can find the thermostat."

The foyer floor was pink-marble-edged with black granite. Sara followed the other woman into the living room, which opened to the left of the foyer. The wall to the right divided the mansion into the two town houses.

"Don't you like it?" Rachel asked.

Realizing she'd been silent too long, Sara put on her brightest smile and nodded. "What's not to like?"

She made a sweeping gesture of the place. The walls and velvet curtains were pale coral, the trim and crown molding glossy white, the accent color black. The colors were taken from a Chinese vase, which was about four feet tall and stood on a black pedestal, with ornately carved balls for legs, to one side of the fireplace. The vase was a mosaic of peaceful garden scenes.

The twenty-foot ceiling was interrupted by a loft that jutted halfway across the room and housed a collection of books and Chinese art in green and pink jade in its wall-to-wall bookcases. Access to the loft was by a library ladder attached to a brass railing with brass rings on the top end.

The loft had a black wrought-iron railing across it with a gate that at present was open. The ladder could be pushed against the far wall when it wasn't needed.

"Clever," Sara said, then surveyed the rest of the room. She didn't think she would ever sit on the velvet sofa of deep coral with shiny, black wood trim. Ebony, maybe? Or Chinese lacquer? She wasn't sure about the wood.

End tables and a coffee table were also black and inlaid with ivory birds and jade bamboo. A collection of Chinese puzzle boxes was displayed in a glass cabinet that had a lock on it. The carpet looked Oriental.

"This looks too expensive to use," she murmured to the other teacher. Rachel's one-bedroom flat, where Sara had gone upon arriving in town that morning, didn't compare to the opulence of this place.

"I agree. The kitchen and den are through here," Rachel told her. "They're more comfortable."

White cabinets on either side of the fireplace had glass doors opening to both the living room and the kitchen. Fine china and more collectibles were inside.

The kitchen had black granite counters. The cabinets were white. The coral walls continued in here as did the oak floors that were stained rather dark for her taste.

Not that anybody would ask her.

Once she'd lived in a mansion only a few miles from this neighborhood, but that had been years ago. She'd been in junior kindergarten herself back then. Back before her father mysteriously disappeared, presumably drowned, from a yacht off the coast of California. Back before her family had lost its diamond-trading and jewelry business. She pushed the bitter thoughts aside as she continued the inspection of her new, albeit temporary, home.

The stainless-steel appliances stood in modern contrast to the Oriental feel of the town house. Between the kitchen and den was a small, formal dining room—table and chairs in the shiny black wood, two vases holding peacock plumes, Chinese scrolls with black lettering on the walls.

"Ah," Sara said, entering the den, "this is lovely."

While the floors and walls repeated the Oriental theme, the sofa was leather and two easy chairs were covered in fabric, all in earthy browns and tans. Tiny figurines carved in jade, onyx and ivory were displayed in another small glass case hung on one wall. There was a fireplace in here, too, one that obviously had been used. A staircase led to the two second-story bedrooms.

"Here's the television and stereo equipment." Rachel opened the door of a built-in cabinet. "And the thermostat. What temperature do you like?"

"Sixty-eight."

"Brr, that's too cold for me, but you probably still have antifreeze in your blood, coming from Colorado."

Sara had grown up counting every penny. Her family had been frugal about utilities and food and clothing out of need, but she didn't say any of this. She heard a soft click, then the gentle stir of air in the room. "Well," she said. "I'd better settle in. It looks like rain."

Rachel shook her head. "Not at this time of the year. That's just the morning fog. It'll burn off by noon."

It was Wednesday, the last day of June, and a cool sixty-two degrees. On Monday, July the fifth, she would start her teaching job at Lakeside. It had been pure luck that the former teacher had taken maternity leave for the year just when Sara had contacted Rachel about a position.

They brought in her clothing and the few household items she'd packed in her ancient compact car. She decided to leave her dishes and pans in their box and store them in the closet. In less than two hours, they were finished.

"Let's go to lunch," Rachel suggested. "There's a Chinese place on the next block that's wonderful. I love their noodle bowls."

Sara shut and locked the door behind them. The

sun broke through the low cloud cover as she joined her friend on the sidewalk. The city was bathed in bright warmth, and she felt comforted, as if the sunlight was a benediction on her and her quest for the truth behind her father's death.

And vengeance for all her family had suffered?

Maybe she could find a way. With her brother's help. Tyler was a detective with the SFPD. They would work together to solve the mysteries from their past.

The first thing Cade noticed upon arriving home that evening was an older model compact car in the driveway of the adjoining town house. Hmm, his neighbor was supposed to be in the Far East, studying the Chinese art he found so fascinating. Who was at the house?

He would investigate, but first he needed to check in with Stacy and Tai. After pulling into the garage, he dashed up the short flight of steps and into the kitchen.

Five-year-old Stacy and her sitter were in the middle of dinner preparations. "Now stir," Stacy ordered.

Tai stirred the contents in the mixing bowl. She was twenty-one and a student at the nearby medical school. She picked up Stacy at day care every afternoon and stayed with her until Cade got home. She prepared dinner for the three of them, too. At times, his arrival was very late, but Tai never complained. She used the time to study.

Cade paused at the door and smiled. Sometimes he wondered who was the boss in this household, but then he knew—it was Stacy.

"Daddy!" she squealed when she saw him. "We're making a cake. It's a surprise."

He closed his eyes. "I won't look," he promised.

She giggled. "It isn't for you," she informed him. "It's for Sara."

"Sara?" Cade glanced at Tai.

"She's your new neighbor. Stacy and I found her weeding the flower bed in front of the house when we got home."

"That explains the strange car in the drive over there," he said. "I didn't know Ron planned on renting the place while he was gone. He usually doesn't trust anyone with his stuff."

"She's a friend of a friend," Tai explained.

"She's sitting the house," Stacy added, then covered her mouth as she giggled over this.

"A house-sitter, huh?" He swung his daughter off the kitchen stool and into the air. She squealed again, this time in laughter as her baby-fine hair swirled out in a blond pouf. After a couple of spins he stopped, then they rubbed noses. Stacy had seen a movie featuring an Eskimo family and learned this was the way they kissed.

"She's pretty," Stacy confided when they were

through with the ritual greeting. "Her hair is dark like Tai's, but her eyes are the color of Mrs. Chong's."

Mrs. Chong was a very fat, very green-eyed cat belonging to Mrs. Ling, who owned the local ice-cream shop. Cade and Stacy were frequent customers.

"Do we have enough dinner to invite her over?" he asked the sitter.

"Sure," Tai answered. "There's a meatball and green bean casserole, roasted potatoes and salad, all ready. I've got to run. I'm memorizing bones this week."

"I'm memering them, too," Stacy declared importantly.

"Memorizing," he automatically corrected. His daughter didn't let pronunciation get in the way of her expressing herself. "Shall we go over and invite our neighbor to eat with us?"

"Yes, but we don't have the surprise cake done yet."

"Maybe she'll help us finish it."

"See you tomorrow," Tai said and headed out.

Cade took her place at the mixing bowl. After he put the cake pans in the oven at Stacy's direction, he set the timer, then held out his hand. "Let's go meet our neighbor."

"I already met her."

"Good, then you can introduce us."

They went out the front door and rang the doorbell to the other town house. In a couple of seconds, Cade saw a blurry figure hurrying to the door.

"Come in—oh!" the most gorgeous creature he'd ever seen called out gaily as she swung open the door, then visibly started when she saw him.

Although Stacy had warned him their new neighbor was pretty, no words could do justice to that combination of black hair and green eyes, the eyes offset to perfection by a sweep of black lashes.

She was average in height and had the type of lithe slenderness he liked in a woman—a long-legged coltish appearance but curvy in the right places, as revealed by a jade-green outfit made of soft clingy material.

For a second, he was speechless as they stared at each other. Then emotion rippled across her face... shock? pain? anger?...he wasn't sure.

No, he must be mistaken, for now she was smiling in a polite manner, then warmer as she glanced at Stacy, a question in her eyes.

"Sorry," he said. "I'm Cade Parks, Stacy's dad. You must be expecting someone...." He let the words trail off into a question.

"No," she said quickly. "Not really. Uh, I'm Sara Carlton, the new kindergarten teacher at Lakeside. Tai says Stacy will be one of my students when classes start."

"Sara, come to our house," Stacy invited. "We're making a surprise for you."

"You must call her Miss Carlton," Cade said.

"Do I have to?" Stacy immediately asked her new teacher.

"Yes, for as long as I'm your teacher."

Stacy nodded in understanding.

"Tai says there's enough food for a guest. We would be honored if you would have dinner with us," Cade told the lovely woman who stood at the door as if guarding the place. "And Stacy has prepared a surprise."

The neighbor smiled.

Oddly, his heart started thumping. Heat gathered low in his body. Other than casual dates, he hadn't had time for a woman since his wife died in a car crash two years ago. All his energy had been expended on his child and his work.

"I never could resist a surprise," the neighbor said. "Let me get my keys."

Stacy went into the house, although they hadn't been invited. Cade stepped into the foyer, too.

"Let's lock the front door," he called after Sara, liking the way she moved, an almost catlike grace in her form as she stopped by a table where her purse sat. "We can go in through the back."

When she nodded, he turned the dead bolt on the ornate front door, then followed as Stacy ran in front to walk with her new teacher. His gaze stayed fastened on the alluring sway of her body as she shortened her steps and took his daughter's hand. Stacy chatted nonstop down the hall, out the back door, onto the shared deck and into their home.

The scent of the baking cake filled the town house,

welcoming the three of them inside. "Mmm, is that the surprise I smell?" Sara asked.

"It's a chocolate cake," Stacy told her, unable to hold the secret inside anymore.

"My favorite," Sara said, her eyes going wide. "How did you know?"

Stacy grinned. "Because it's mine and Daddy's, too."

Their laughter flowed over and into him, adding to the intimacy of the moment. Observing their guest as he removed plates from the cabinet, he wondered if they had met before.

He felt as if they had. In another life, perhaps. Perhaps they'd been lovers, separated by some tragic fate, but destined to meet again….

A surge of need so great, it was almost a pain rolled over him. He'd never felt anything like it, not even when he fell for his wife. Rita Lambini was the deb of the season six years ago, a beautiful socialite who'd enchanted him with her smoldering glances and flirty, laughing ways.

That hadn't lasted long.

In less than six months, the enchantment was gone, leaving the bitter knowledge that she'd married him for the money he'd inherit one day. He'd wanted out of the marriage, but she'd been pregnant by then.

Recalling his own past, with his mother in a Swiss sanitarium due to health reasons and his father only interested in the diamond business, Cade had known he couldn't leave his child fatherless. So he'd stuck it out until Stacy was born.

Watching his daughter come into the world, he'd felt nothing but love at first sight. And it had stayed that way.

Rita, knowing she now had a weapon, had fought the divorce and threatened a lengthy custody battle. She'd even hinted she would accuse him of child abuse if he tried to kick her out.

He still felt guilty over the relief her death had brought. She'd been returning from one of her many social affairs…a few drinks and the winding, fog-slick coastal road coupled with fast driving had ended at a curve with a fifty-foot cliff on the other side. Rita had crashed through the barrier and gone over the edge—

"Daddy!" Stacy tugged at his arm.

He realized she'd been speaking to him. "Sorry, what did you say?"

"We're ready. Sar—Miss Carlton and I set the table."

Seeing those green eyes watching him with a curious expression in their depths, he shrugged off the past and smiled at the other two. "Good job."

The timer buzzed just then. He removed the cake layers from the oven and put in three dinner rolls to brown while they started on the salad course.

"Is this your first teaching position?" he asked when they were seated.

"Uh, no. I taught for almost five years in Denver."

"So what brought you to San Francisco?"

Her hesitation was noticeable. "I have friends here," she said. "They arranged things for me."

Disappointment hit him. "A boyfriend?"

She glanced at him, then shook her head. "A fellow teacher, actually. She's a friend of a friend of the artist who owns the other town house."

"Miss Hanson," Stacy informed her father.

"Yes. Rachel and my…"

Again the pause, as if she wasn't sure if she should disclose this much, Cade noted.

"Rachel and my brother thought I needed to get away."

"From Denver?" he asked.

She nodded.

"Why?" He realized he sounded like a lawyer before the court, trying to wring information from a witness.

"My…my mother died after a long illness. In the winter. She loved the spring in Colorado and the wildflowers. She used to say flowers and children were the only consolations life offered."

This last part was said with such sadness, Cade felt like a heel for making her speak of it. "I've caused you pain," he said. "I'm sorry."

"No, no, it's okay." Her smile bloomed once more. "I thought it was time for a change, too. Meeting Stacy today convinced me this move was the right thing."

Again he had an overwhelming sensation of déjà

vu, as if they'd talked like this before, as if they'd shared secrets, laughed together. It was damned odd.

"The rolls are ready," Stacy announced.

Cade served the rest of the meal, then they opened a can of chocolate icing and finished the cake. "Let's sing Happy Birthday," Stacy requested.

"It isn't anyone's birthday," he reminded his daughter.

"Mine was back in the spring," Sara told them. "No one made me a cake, so this can be a belated one."

He thought of all she didn't say—her grief over her mother, the loneliness in those eyes, the fragile quality that brought out something protective in him.

"Great," he said. "Stacy, start us off."

Stacy began. "Happy birthday to you…"

He joined in, harmonizing with her childish soprano. Their guest looked at him in surprise. He smiled, pleased that he'd managed to break through the reserve that surrounded her.

"How old are you?" Stacy demanded while he cut the cake, then served their guest first.

"Twenty-nine."

"Stace, you're not supposed to ask a woman her age," he chided.

"Why?" she asked.

"Yes, why?" Sara echoed.

He pretended to think. "Darned if I know," he finally said. "Someone told me it was rude, that women don't like admitting how old they are."

"We don't mind being old, do we, Sar—Miss Carlton?"

"Not at all. Age makes one wiser, I've heard."

A full, unforced smile appeared on her sensuous lips. Cade couldn't take his gaze from them. "I've seen that smile before," he said. "Where have we met?"

Sara was unprepared for the question or his intent perusal. After twenty-five years, she hadn't expected him to make any connection to her at all. She tried to maintain the smile, but it was impossible.

"Long ago," she said in a low voice, "we were in kindergarten together. You and I and your twin sister, Emily. Here, in San Francisco."

His eyes narrowed as he stared at her. "Yes," he said after a thoughtful silence. "Sara Carlton. Yes. That explains the eyes. And the smile. I knew I'd seen them somewhere. I had a terrible crush on you. Then one day you left without a word. I was heartbroken."

"We moved away."

He nodded. "I remember. Your father died. A boating accident or something," Cade said.

Or something, Sara echoed to herself, that *something* being the murder of her father by his. She bit the words back with an effort. She hated subterfuge and lies, but in this case it was necessary.

"A hard year for you," he murmured. "For everyone," he added on an introspective note.

His smile was sad as well as sympathetic. She

knew his mother had been sent away "for health reasons" later that same year.

She rejected pity for him and his family. After all, she was here for revenge....

No, it was justice she sought. She was here to see that Walter Parks paid for his crime.

Chapter Two

Sara sat on the sofa in the den Thursday night and watched a bead of moisture gather, then meander down the window, gaining speed as it collected more water.

No rain fell. With darkness, the fog had rolled in off the ocean and tumbled over the low hills like spirits released on the unsuspecting city folk. It condensed on the panes and formed the droplets.

Inside, she had a fire going in the grate, which held artificial logs, the flames fed with gas rather than wood. But it was still cozy and cheerful.

She needed cheering.

During the day, her first full one in the city, she'd

kept busy. There'd been groceries to buy and errands to run, then she'd walked over to Lakeside School for the Gifted to be sure she could find it come Monday.

The private school was housed in elegant brick quarters, which had been a donation from the school's founder in memory of his son, much as Stanford University had been established.

On her walk along St. Francis Boulevard, she'd passed the California Scottish Rite Temple and a forest preserve called the Sigmund Stern Grove. Directly across the street from the preserve, she'd found the school.

She'd also discovered that street names often changed at a cross street for no discernible reason. Junipero Serra became Portola Drive which became Market Street as it neared downtown. However, the area was interesting and lovely, with the ocean, several parks and golf courses, plus three universities within a two-mile radius of her temporary home.

Like Rome, San Francisco was built on hills. Mt. Davidson at nine hundred and twenty-seven feet was the highest peak in the vicinity while Twin Peaks, a short distance north of it, was next at nine hundred and ten feet. They were nothing like the rocky, snow-covered crags near her old home in Colorado.

During the fall and winter, she'd often sat for hours and gazed at those lofty spires as she'd waited for her mother's life to be over....

"Sara?" the feeble voice said in a whisper.

"Yes, Mom?" Sara rose from the hospital chair, which also made a bed, and went to her mother's side. It was the day after Christmas.

Marla Carlton gazed intently at her daughter. "You remember everything I told you? Kathleen and the twins...they know, don't they?"

Sara took her mother's restless hand. It felt like a skeleton's, it was so thin and bony now. "Yes, they know. We all know."

"Find my brother. Find Derek."

"He's here, Mother. He arrived this morning. He'll be back at visiting hours."

"He knows...he saw...everything."

"Shh, don't talk. Rest now," Sara urged.

It hurt to look at her mother. The vestiges of her former beauty were still visible. Full, sensuous lips. An enchanting smile. Black hair threaded with gray but still thick and luxurious. Green eyes with long black lashes. A petite, lovely Cleopatra once, she was ravaged by illness more than time. At fifty-five she was dying of heart disease and there was nothing the doctors could do.

Pain speared through Sara at the thought. As the oldest of her siblings, she'd taken on the responsibility for the family during her growing years. Their mom had never been well. Depression and dark moods had plagued her.

Now Sara understood why. Marla had carried a horrible burden in her heart for twenty-five years, ever since her husband had disappeared from a yacht off the coast of California. Now Sara understood why she and her sister were snatched from their familiar world in San Francisco and taken to Denver to a life of struggle and uncertainty.

"Derek was there," Marla said, clutching Sara's hand as if to hold her captive to the tale the daughter had already heard more than once of late. "He saw Walter...."

Sara bent close as her mother's eyes closed and her words lapsed into agitated mumbling. The story she'd heard during the past week had been a strange, terrifying Christmas gift—a disclosure of greed, murder and ruin visited on her father by the man who was supposed to be his friend and business partner in the diamond trade.

Walter Parks.

The name conjured up unspeakable evil in her mind as she stared into her mother's pale face. The man had threatened Marla with her life if she didn't disappear from San Francisco forever. He'd threatened the lives of her children, Sara and Kathleen, too. He hadn't known Marla had been pregnant with the twins, Tyler and Conrad.

Or that those two unborn babies were his—

The ring of the doorbell startled Sara out of the painful memories. It was almost nine o'clock. Maybe her brother was making an appearance at last. She'd expected him yesterday.

"About time," she scolded when she opened the door and saw that it was indeed Tyler.

He was still in the suit he wore as a detective with the police department. Giving her a grin, he swept her into a bear hug.

It never failed to amaze her that the twins she'd adored—at five, she'd thought they were some sort of living dolls made especially for her—had grown into men, six feet tall with broad shoulders and muscular bodies.

"Oomph," she said to let him know he was squeezing the breath out of her.

"Sorry, sis," he said, not at all apologetic. "God, it seems like years. I'm glad you're here."

"Me, too. I think."

Their eyes met in grave acknowledgment of the task they'd set for themselves before leaving Denver—find their uncle, sole witness to the crime against their family, then present the case to the local district attorney.

"The den is through here." She led the way.

His low whistle told her he was as impressed by the town house as she'd been. Tyler had arrived in town a few months ago, landed a job as a police detective and found a best friend in Nick Banning, his partner on the force.

Nick was responsible for the connections that had led to her living in the town house, right next door to

Cade Parks, son of the man they were after. Step Two of their plan was now in action.

The first step had been for both of them to get jobs here. The second had been to find a way to infiltrate the Parks family. What better way than to live next door to the oldest son, who was also the Parks family attorney?

"Pretty nice digs," Tyler said, settling in one of the easy chairs before the hearth. "You should see the place Nick found for me."

His wry laughter dispelled any impression of envy. Her baby brother didn't waste time on useless emotions.

"Irish coffee?" she asked. "There's a latte machine, if you'd prefer that."

"Can you make it both?"

Sara foamed nonfat milk into fresh coffee, then added a generous splash of Irish cream liqueur. After placing a stirring stick coated with brown sugar crystals in each tall mug, she carried them into the den where Tyler waited, his eyes, green like hers, fixed on the flames leaping over the fake logs.

Marla had left her stamp on all her children, bequeathing her black hair and cat eyes to each of them, along with a megawatt smile and a metabolism that enabled them to eat anything and stay thin, a fact their friends often lamented.

"Have you met your neighbor?" Tyler asked.

Sara was drawn out of her introspection. "Yes,

yesterday. Cade's daughter, Stacy, is friendly and in-
quisitive. As soon as she saw me weeding the front
yard, she came over and demanded to know if I was
the new gardener and what had happened to Mr.
Lee.''

"Cade?" Tyler questioned, at once picking up on
the use of the first name.

"He and Stacy had me over for dinner last night.
They made a surprise cake. And sang happy birthday
to me.''

Tyler muttered an expletive. "I forgot about your
birthday.''

"That's okay. Some friends in Denver took me out
for a gala celebration.''

"You've lost weight. Is this going to be too hard
on you? Nick and I can handle the investigation.''

"No, no. I want to do it. I want to find out the truth
about our father and his partner.''

When Tyler's eyes flicked to her with more than a
little irony in their depths, she recalled *her* father
wasn't *his* father. She still found it hard to believe
that the man they sought to bring to justice was father
to the twins.

"Dear God, what a mess, if this is all true," she
murmured.

"Didn't you believe Mother's story?" he asked in
his blunt fashion. His gaze bored into her as if he
dared her to deny it. Tyler was always direct.

"Yes, but we can't prove anything without finding

the uncle I don't recall ever seeing until just before her death. How did he know she was sick? He had to have been keeping track of her somehow. Could they have corresponded all these years and Mother never told us?''

''Who knows? Mother could be as silent as a sphinx when she chose. Derek Ross is one hell of an elusive relative,'' Tyler admitted. ''All I could find out was that after the funeral his flight from Denver ended in San Francisco. He isn't listed on the Internet or in any telephone book, hasn't been called to jury duty, gotten any traffic tickets or been delinquent on his taxes that I can find.''

''I was thinking of those last days in the hospital earlier tonight, just before you arrived, in fact,'' Sara said in a pensive tone. ''We all reacted differently.''

''Yeah,'' Tyler agreed in disgust. ''Kathleen, the mystery writer, ran away to New York after the funeral. You would think solving a twenty-five-year-old mystery would be right up her alley.''

''And Conrad wouldn't budge from Colorado. They both want justice, but they act as if they're in denial about the whole situation.'' She stirred the latte, then took a sip of the hot brew, feeling its warmth flow all the way to her tummy.

''It's pretty hard to realize the man you thought was your father *wasn't* in actuality. And that the man who is really your sire killed the one you thought *was*.

Man, try explaining all that to a jury,'' he finished grimly.

''Are you going to confront Walter Parks about your paternity?''

''Yes.''

''When?''

''Soon. I want to see the bastard's reaction when he realizes his sins have come back to haunt him.''

''Tyler, be careful. He's killed once—''

''That we know of,'' Tyler interrupted.

''It's probably easier the second time,'' she warned. Anger and grief brought tears to her eyes. ''Sometimes I'm so filled with hate,'' she said. ''Other times, I think it might be better to go away and forget everything. It was so far in the past and there are so many innocent people who may be hurt by bringing it into the open.''

Tyler studied her for a long minute. ''Like your neighbor?'' He gestured toward the town house in the other side of the duplex.

''Like his little girl.''

''Why should they get off scot-free?'' he demanded. ''Our family didn't. Justice will be done.'' He slapped the ball of his fist down on his knee.

Tension filled the beautiful town house which had been arranged in *feng shui* fashion for the maximum tranquillity of the human soul.

''Justice can be harsh,'' she murmured. ''There's

an ancient Chinese saying that sounds as if it's a blessing, but it's really a curse.''

''What's that?'' he asked when she paused.

'''May you live in interesting times.' To the sages, interesting times were those filled with chaos and troubles. Their greatest wish was for serenity. I think, little brother, that we're in for some interesting times.''

He finished the drink and stood as the clock on the mantel chimed ten times. ''Good. We'll see who's standing when the Parks house of cards comes tumbling down.''

After she saw him out, watching as his taillights disappeared around a corner, Sara stood at the door for another minute. Down the street, the fog encircled the streetlight in a dim haze. The faint glow gave the promise of warmth and succor to the lone man who walked toward it with quick strides. He paused at the corner and looked over his shoulder, then hurried on.

She wondered what demons he feared might come after him out of the swirling dampness of the night.

On Friday, Sara reacquainted herself with the city. Not that she remembered much from twenty-five years ago, but she tried. She visited the zoo and took the scenic drive in a loop around the city and surrounding urban streets.

One of the two windmills near the old Cliff House spa resort had been restored. The fresh and saltwater pools had long fallen into ruins, but the house remained, having been rebuilt a couple of times due to fire. She ate lunch at the restaurant and knew she'd eaten there in her childhood, although she couldn't dredge up a specific occasion. Perhaps someone's birthday.

Past the windmill, facing the ocean, the houses were being gentrified. New construction was going on in the area. None of that was familiar to her.

However, another neighborhood, down the Great Pacific Coast Highway toward Half Moon Bay, brought back sharp, poignant memories. There, in an expensive enclave of homes on five-acre estates carved from sage brush and artichoke farms, she located her former home with the help of an address she'd found in her mother's possessions.

Standing at the locked gate of the imposing but run-down mansion, images flooded her mind. She'd been riding a tricycle on the sidewalk. Her father was yelling for her to stop as she gained speed on the downward slope. She'd shot through the open wrought-iron gates and gone off the curb in a tangle of arms, legs and tricycle wheels and had a terrific crash on the pavement.

Her parents had taken her to the emergency room for a broken collarbone. She'd tried not to cry, but it had been the worst pain she'd ever experienced.

Running her fingers over the long-repaired bone, she reviewed her life since that time. Her mother's fears. Her weeping. Moving from one cheap apartment to another. Settling at last in Denver. Her own childish delight in the snow, which she'd never seen, and the birth of the twins. Another delight for her, but more pain for her mother.

The mansion was unoccupied and in disrepair. The old man who had bought it by paying the back taxes had lived here alone after his wife died. He'd passed away a few years ago, and his children were in a battle over the property, according to Tyler. So the place sat empty and forlorn, looking like an aging beauty waiting for her fickle bridegroom to return and make things right again.

"May I help you?" a voice asked, startling her.

A policeman had stopped at the curb and called to her from the open window of his cruiser. A stab of fear hit her. She reminded herself she wasn't doing anything wrong.

Sara shook her head. "I used to live here. A long time ago," she added when he looked skeptical. "Since I was in the city, I decided to see if I could remember the place."

"This house has been empty a long time. I try to keep an eye on it. An unoccupied house is an invitation for drug dealers to move in."

"That would be terrible."

"You had better move on," he told her, but in a kind manner. "Your staring has made the lady down the street nervous. She reported someone was 'casing' the estate. That's why I came by.''

''I'm sorry. I didn't mean to cause trouble,'' Sara told the officer.

She walked back to her car, parked at the curb near where she'd fallen so many years ago. She felt close to tears as the nostalgic mood lingered.

Heading for the town house in her old but dependable vehicle, she had to laugh. Obviously she and her family had fallen on leaner times since their days in the mansion. The policeman would probably tell his fellow cops about the encounter and spend the afternoon painting scenarios of what had happened to them. Someone at the station might even recall the disappearance of Jeremy Carlton and the mystery surrounding his death, presumably by drowning, but the body was never found.

Sara had questions of her own. What had happened to her father's business? His money? How had her mother managed with four children and no job?

The latter was answered when she and Tyler had discovered funds in a brokerage account after their mother's death. She'd lived very frugally off the interest, using extra money only during emergencies.

Sara thought her mom would have been better off if she'd had to work, to get out and interact with people so that she wouldn't spend hours alone in the tiny rental house where they'd finally settled in a suburb of Denver.

At the town house, she pulled into the short driveway and turned off the engine. Stacy was sitting on the marble stoop, chin in her hands, elbows propped on her knees. She smiled broadly when Sara came up the walk.

"I ringed...rang your doorbell but you weren't home," she said, moving over so Sara could sit.

Sara enjoyed the coolness of the stone through her slacks as she joined the child. By midafternoon the temperature had climbed into the upper seventies and the shade of the alcove was nice after her day of exploration.

"I've been on the scenic tour of the city," she told Stacy. "I saw Fisherman's Wharf and the Golden Gate Bridge and had lunch at Cliff House. My table was by the window so I could see the ocean."

"Did you see any ships?"

"Yes. A huge one. It looked like an oceangoing barge."

She was rocked by a sudden image of herself at four. She was standing by a window and looking out at the sea, wondering where her daddy could be and why he'd gone off on a boat and when he was going to come back.

With grave certainty, she knew she'd been looking out the window of her bedroom in the mansion—

"Do you have a headache?" Stacy asked.

Sara dropped her hand—she'd been unconsciously

rubbing her temple—into her lap. "No, just thinking." She smiled to show she was all right.

"My mommy used to have headaches. She'd tell Daddy to leave her alone, she had a headache—whenever he was mad at her."

Sara was startled by the grown-up words coming from the child's mouth. Surely Stacy had been too young to remember what sounded like frequent quarrels between her parents.

But maybe not. Vague recollections were coming back to her from her youth now that she had returned.

A premonition that she and Tyler should leave the past behind and get on with their lives pierced her heart like a hot spear. Surely there had been enough unhappiness back then to last all of them a lifetime.

Looking at young Stacy, Sara wondered if bringing the ancient case up, assuming they found their missing uncle and solved the murder, was worth it in light of the pain it might cause innocents like this child.

"Daddy!" Stacy yelled, jumping up and running to the end of the sidewalk.

Cade Parks pulled into the garage on his side of the house, then joined his daughter, coming through the gate and scooping her into his arms. "What are you doing sitting out front? You know you're not supposed to do that."

"Tai said I could wait for you. You're late," Stacy said, turning the reprimand on him.

Sara couldn't help but grin. She wouldn't say the

daughter was smarter than her dad, but she certainly had learned the rudiments of outfoxing the main male in her life. Sara pitied the men in Stacy's social circle when the little scamp grew up.

"Huh," her dad said, then added, "Sorry I'm late. Grandpa called at the last minute. You know how hard it is to get off the line when he wants information."

Grandpa. That would be Walter Parks. Well, Stacy did have another grandfather, but according to Tyler, the families didn't mingle much, except for delivering the girl for an occasional visit.

Stacy giggled, then held her face up. To Sara's amusement, the big city lawyer solemnly rubbed noses with his daughter, then settled on the steps with her in his lap.

"Nice out today," he said.

"Yes."

"Did you go sightseeing?"

"Actually, I did."

Tai came out the front door. "I'm off to the library. See you Monday, pie face," she said to Stacy, leaning down to plant a kiss on the child's forehead.

"The office will be closed Monday since the fourth is on Sunday this year," Cade reminded the sitter, "so you don't have to pick her up until Tuesday."

"Ah, that'll give me more time to study." Looking pleased, the medical student rushed off with a back-pack of books swinging from her shoulders, her long straight hair bouncing against it with each hurried stride.

"I don't know what I would do without her," Cade murmured as Stacy followed Tai, then swung on the gate after waving to her sitter. "She's totally dependable."

"When I was little, I tried to eat a whole pie by myself," Stacy called to Sara from the gate. "Tai took my picture. It's so funny."

Sara observed the warmth in Cade's smile as he nodded in agreement with Stacy's story. She could remember her father coming home and sweeping her and baby sister Kathleen into his arms for a big kiss, then bending their mother over his arm for a dramatic Hollywood embrace. They'd all laughed at how funny he was.

"What?" Cade asked, bending his head so he could look into her eyes.

"I beg your pardon?"

"You looked so sad there for a minute."

Sara realized she needed to be more careful about concealing her feelings. "Not at all. I was just thinking about how good you are with Stacy and how I wish other fathers were as involved with their families."

He was silent for several seconds. "I want to be different from my father. It has always been obvious to us kids that his business came first."

"I remember your twin sister, Emily. Are there others in your family?"

Tyler had already told her about the Parks family, but Sara thought it better to feign ignorance.

"Two. Jessica is an artist. Her paintings are becoming known and beginning to sell. And there's another boy, Rowan. He's the wild one in the family. He drives the old man crazy with some of his stunts."

"Such as?" Sara asked, unable to suppress her interest.

"Tearing around on a motorcycle. Having his picture plastered all over the newspaper in a compromising position with a politician's wife. Just the everyday rebellions of a middle child who got little attention."

"You're the 'good' son," she concluded. "The oldest, who is expected to step into the father's shoes when the family patriarch decides it's time."

Cade hesitated, then chuckled. "Except I went into law instead of the diamond business."

"Why?"

"I like the purity of it, the fairness—"

"Not always," she interrupted, thinking of her quest. "There have been innocents on death row."

"Well, I'm speaking of the idealism of the law, not the reality of its execution by mankind."

She found herself laughing with him, his deeper tones like the mellow notes of a bassoon underplaying her higher fluting ones.

"Stace and I are grilling hamburgers tonight. Want to join us?"

She hesitated. "I imposed on you night before last."

"It's no imposition. We like the company. Besides, knowing you will make Stace feel more confident when she starts school at Lakeside."

Sara couldn't help it. She started to laugh.

"What?" he demanded. He nudged her shoulder with his.

His smile was brilliant against his somewhat swarthy complexion, inherited from some pirate ancestor, Sara decided as her breath quickened at his playful touch. His eyes were hazel, a fascinating mix of brown and green with golden flecks near the pupil.

"If Stacy gets any more confident, she'll be running the class and I'll be sitting in the corner for talking while she's explaining the lesson plan." Sara gave him a sardonic glance from under her lashes. "I think it's her daddy who's worried about school."

A sigh escaped him. "Day care is one thing. Real school is something else, even if it is kindergarten," he admitted. "It's like she'll be taking on a whole new life, one that doesn't involve me. I've cared for her since she was born. Now someone else will influence her, maybe have a greater impact on her life. Next thing I know, she'll be dragging some boy home and announcing marriage plans."

He swiped a hand over his brow in an exaggerated

fashion, causing her to laugh again. The gate clanged merrily as Stacy swung on it and hummed a song.

"Well, you do have a few years to get used to the idea of marriage and all that," Sara said ruefully, unsympathetic to the woeful picture he painted.

"Thank God. Come on, let's get those hamburgers on. Stacy requested them especially for you. She said they were your favorite food."

"Next to chocolate cake. Is there any of that left?"

"You bet." He stood and offered her a hand.

Sara let him help her up, then when he called the child to them, they all went to the back deck to eat. Later they watched the sun set far out on the horizon.

"Look for the green flash," Cade said, peering intently toward the sea.

"What's that?" Sara wanted to know.

"In the instant the sun dips below the ocean, there's a green flash, so quick you'll miss it if you blink. If you see it, you'll have good luck. Ah, there it is. Did you see?"

"I did," Stacy declared. "Did you?" she asked, looking at Sara with hazel eyes that exactly matched her father's.

Sara nodded. Amazingly, she had. She really had.

Chapter Three

One way to get information was to insinuate oneself into the informant's life. That was part of the plan when she and Tyler had contrived to get jobs here and find out all they could about the Parks family.

So why, Sara wondered on Sunday evening, did she feel so guilty about accepting another invitation from Cade and Stacy?

Draping a warm sweater over her arm, she slipped her wallet in the pocket of her jeans, looked around for anything she might have forgotten, then went to the front door when the doorbell rang several times.

Stacy stood on the other side, a big grin on her face. Sara returned the smile and felt just miserable. Why did doing the right thing feel so wrong?

Because of this youngster, she answered her own question. Because once she'd been Stacy's age and her world had turned upside down. She'd been bewildered and frightened by her mother's strange behavior.

"Come on," Stacy coached. "We're ready."

"I'm coming." Sara locked the door and followed her young hostess to the expensive sedan parked at the curb with Cade inside and waiting for them.

"We have cookies," Stacy announced, taking her place in a child's safety seat in the back. She expertly buckled herself into the harness.

Sara sat in the front with Cade. Her dealings with them were beginning to feel too intimate.

No, that wasn't the word. They were getting too companionable. As if they were a family.

The plan that had seemed practical and logical in Denver now took on sinister shadings as she interacted with Cade and his daughter. She liked them. Unfortunately, that fact hadn't figured in her planning.

And there was another problem.

She hadn't counted on being physically attracted to him. He was tall, probably eight inches above her own five foot six. He wore his dark-brown hair rather short as befitted an attorney. He looked great in three-piece suits or in jeans, T-shirt and a green corduroy long-sleeved shirt, which was what he was wearing now.

There was a seriousness about him that inspired

confidence, yet his smiles were quick and frequent, especially in dealing with young Stacy. He had a world of patience, yet he could be firm when necessary.

Maybe she should ask Tyler what the contingency plan was if either of them fell head over heels for someone in the Parks family. What then, little brother? she mentally asked with a heavy dose of irony. She couldn't come up with an answer on the short ride to Twin Peaks.

Deep twilight had fallen when Cade stopped by a parking space at the observation point, and the youth who sat there in a lawn chair moved so he could pull in.

"Nothing like having friends in high places," Sara murmured.

"Nothing like having a secretary whose son will do nearly anything for money. He's saving for his first car."

"When will the fireworks start?" Stacy demanded. She unbuckled the seat belt and stood leaning over the front seat between her father and Sara.

"Soon," Cade promised. He glanced at Sara. "Each city along the bay schedules their Fourth of July display one after the other. We'll see at least three different shows from here."

"Mmm, there'll be a lot of tired teachers in school tomorrow," she said. "We have a week of training and orientation before the students arrive."

Cade frowned. "I'm not sure I like this year-round

school idea. Or the idea of moving kids up from the day care center to kindergarten on an irregular schedule.''

''They're moved when the tests show they're ready. Otherwise, they get bored and decide school is no fun.''

''Back in my day, no one thought it was supposed to be fun. It was for learning. Or else,'' he added ominously.

''Yes, but that was in the olden days,'' Sara said tongue-in-cheek. ''Things are different in modern times.''

He burst out laughing. ''That'll teach me to refer to my kindergarten days. But let me remind you— you were in the same class as I was.''

''Daddy, are you as old as Sara?'' Stacy wanted to know.

''Miss Carlton,'' he corrected. ''Yes, we're both as ancient as the hills.''

The girl thought this was extremely funny. Cade glanced at Sara, his eyes alight with amusement. They shared a smile. It was on this humorous note that the fireworks began. They exclaimed over the brilliant exhibitions and argued about which city had the best shots while munching on the homemade cookies Stacy and her dad had made.

Sara sighed contentedly on the way back to the house.

''Tired?'' Cade asked, picking up on the sound.

''Yes, but pleasantly so,'' she said. ''I haven't paid

much attention to holiday celebrations for the last couple of years.''

''Because of your mother's illness?'' he asked softly, his tone sympathetic.

''That was part of it,'' she admitted.

She stared into the darkness as despair returned. The burden of caring for her mom had fallen on her. Kathleen couldn't deal with illness. Or anything else, if she didn't want to. Her sister had been spoiled, but Sara knew it was partly her fault. It had been easier to do everything herself than cajole the other girl into helping.

It had been the same with Conrad. Tyler had taken on the responsibilities of the man of the house as he grew older. Between the two of them, she and Tyler had made most of the decisions involving their family. They had grown close because of it.

''Here we are,'' Cade said, breaking into her musing. ''Stacy's asleep. I'll carry her inside.''

''I can help,'' Sara volunteered.

She opened doors so Cade could carry his daughter inside. In the child's bedroom, Sara watched as he slipped Stacy's coat and shoes off. The child had come dressed in pajamas beforehand. Leaning down, he kissed the smooth forehead and pulled the covers up. He was the most caring man Sara had ever met.

She moved back from the doorway when Cade stepped into the hall and closed the door.

''How about a cup of coffee?'' he asked.

She hesitated. It was close to midnight. A dangerous hour. "All right," she heard herself say and was surprised. She hadn't meant to say that at all.

Downstairs she stood at the kitchen counter which, as in her place, divided it from the hall that connected the living quarters. Cade's town house was much less formal than the one she was in. The walls were sunny yellow in the den, a soft doeskin beige in the kitchen and dining room.

The furniture was old and comfortable. She suspected some of the pieces were antiques. If so, they had been restored to prime condition by an expert hand.

"My brother Rowan refinished that piece and gave it to me and Rita as a wedding gift," Cade said, seeing her gaze on a maple secretary with inlaid rosewood.

"It's lovely."

"It was a surprise," Cade said, his expression rather thoughtful. "I didn't know he knew oak from pine at the time. Now he works as a carpenter and furniture maker."

"People can amaze you," she murmured, thinking of her mother and her secrets.

"There you go again," Cade said softly. "Looking sad," he added when she glanced his way.

"I'm not sad at all," she quickly told him and smiled to prove it.

He said nothing further, but his glance was skeptical. She really had to be more careful of her emotions around him. He saw too much.

When the decaffeinated coffee was ready, they carried the mugs into the den. He turned on the gas long enough to start the wood so they could have a fire.

"You have real logs," she said.

"Yes. I buy a cord from the Boy Scouts each year. For twenty bucks extra, they stack it in the garage, so it's a good deal."

She nodded. "I've wondered what the artist was hiding in his garage. The inside door is locked with a dead bolt, which I don't have a key for."

"Nothing sinister," Cade assured her. "He stores art treasures there until he can move them to his gallery, which is where he sells his paintings as well as imported art."

"I see."

Sara was aware of the silence surrounding them as they watched the flames, each on an opposite end of the sofa. Cade set his mug on the coffee table, then turned so that he leaned into the corner, facing her.

"Sara," he said and took the mug from her trembling hands and set it aside.

Sparks shot along her nerves at the husky tone. She cleared her throat. "Yes?"

He slid along the sofa until he could hook a finger under her chin and turn her face to his. "Just…this," he murmured. Then he kissed her.

His lips were warm and mobile over hers, his touch firm but gentle, filling her with a vast yearning for things that could never be, not between them.

Quick, hot tears pressed behind her closed eyes,

forlorn, useless tears, for all the years and all the sorrows that stood between her and this man. One slipped over her lashes and wended down her cheek.

Laying her hands on his chest, she pressed slightly.

"What bothers you so?" he asked, a puzzled frown forming on his face as he caught the tear on a finger. "Is it me? Or something from your past? Or from our past when we knew each other as children?"

All of the above.

But she didn't say that. "It's been a long time since I've been kissed." She tried to smile but her mouth trembled too much. She pressed her lips together.

"Why?" He bent his head slightly in order to study the expression in her eyes. "Why has it been a long time since you've been kissed?"

She looked away, staring into the flames until she was sure the words would come. "This time last year I went to a party. With my fiancé."

Cade's face disclosed no reaction to her words. "And?"

"We had a quarrel, and he…drove home alone while I had a friend drop me off."

When she paused, Cade nodded and told her to go on.

"He was drinking and I thought he shouldn't drive, but he wouldn't listen, so I…I let him go. He had an accident and…and…"

"He died?" Cade said, supplying the ending to her story.

"Yes. Luckily no other cars were involved. He

wasn't found until around noon the next day. He'd gone off an embankment and the car wasn't visible from the road. A man and his son trying to get to the river to fish happened to see the tire tracks. They found him, but it was too late.''

"I'm sorry,'' Cade said.

He slid his hands into her hair at each temple and held her. He kissed her eyes, each cheek, then the corner of her mouth. Each touch was unbearably tender.

"I should have called the police, or at least threatened to. Maybe he would have listened then. But I didn't. I was angry.''

"It wasn't your fault.'' He licked away the tears that seeped from beneath her closed lashes. ''It wasn't,'' he insisted when she tried to tell him it was. ''We make choices. Sometimes they're the wrong ones. Each person is responsible for his or her decisions, not someone else's.''

He kissed her again, angling across her mouth, seeking greater contact. She pulled away. ''You don't know,'' she whispered. ''You don't know.''

"I do. My wife's car went over a cliff two years ago. I was relieved that she was gone. I felt guilty as hell for feeling that way. I still do. But we have to go on,'' he added on a gentler note. ''You were wise to move here.''

"Wise?'' she questioned, staring into his eyes and wondering why he thought that.

"You've had two tragedies to cope with this past

year. Leaving Denver means you're ready to get on with your life. Stacy and I are very lucky that you decided to come to California.''

She fought the hot rise of tears and managed to hold them in. ''I wonder if you'll feel that way a year from now,'' she said, then stood and hurried out the back door and into the sanctuary of her house.

After locking the door, she stood in the dark with her forehead pressed against the wooden panel and listened to the frantic pounding of her heart. She wasn't moving forward with her life, but going backward, she wanted to tell Cade.

Twenty-five years, to be exact.

Sara's first week at Lakeside was spent in meetings with the administration, going over schedules and class plans. She marked holidays and vacations in her day planner. Her friend Rachel had a PDA, a small electronic device which had a calendar, address book and several other functions.

''I'm going to save up and get one of those,'' Sara declared at lunch on Friday.

The teachers' orientation program had ended at noon and they were free the rest of the day. The two had opted to go to the nearby Chinese restaurant in celebration.

Rachel agreed. ''With the school on a year-round program, it's a great help. Otherwise, I can never keep up with student holidays, when we teachers have to work, versus school holidays, when the whole place is closed down." She smiled past Sara's shoulder. "Well, hi, there," she said. "It's a really good-looking guy," she said to Sara.

Sara glanced behind her. "Tyler, hello," she said in surprise. She hadn't heard a word from him all week.

"Hey, sis. Hello, Rachel. Nice seeing you again," he said, joining them at their table. "I've been looking for you two."

"How did you find us?" Sara asked, feeling only slightly apprehensive at his remark. His manner was relaxed, so she assumed he brought no compelling news.

"I stopped at the school and asked. The gal in the office said she thought you were coming here." When the waiter appeared, Tyler ordered the day's noodle bowl special, then glanced at the two women. "Nick and I have tomorrow night off. How about dinner and a movie? We'll spring for both of you since cops make a lot more money than teachers."

"Now that's an offer I for one can't refuse," Sara murmured in amusement at her brother's sardonic style. "How about it, Rachel?"

Her friend considered. "We could hold out for a better deal. The hot dog guy down at Fisherman's Wharf makes more than cops, I think. But," she added quickly, "he isn't nearly as handsome. What time are you two big spenders picking us up? Or shall we meet you somewhere?"

Tyler grinned. ''Can you be at Sara's place at six? We'll eat early and catch the eight-o'clock show.''

After they finished their lunch, Tyler went back on duty. Sara and Rachel decided to spend the afternoon window-shopping. ''There's a place I want to go,'' Sara said when they exited a department store in Union Square.

''Parks,'' Rachel said, understanding at once. ''It's down this way.''

Sara found her heart speeding up when they stopped to look in the window at the top-line jewelry. Entering the showroom, she felt like a sneak thief, as if she was there for nefarious purposes.

''May I help you?'' a smartly dressed woman asked.

She wore a black suit with a black silk camisole and a necklace of the largest pearls Sara had ever seen. The necklace and earrings were set off to perfection by the fairness of the woman's skin and the darkness of her hair and suit. Her eyes were very pale blue-gray.

''We're just looking,'' Rachel said breezily, her tone implying they might buy something if anything struck their fancy.

The woman smiled, nodded and faded into the background.

Sara glanced around the store. It was as exquisite as the woman, done in subtle tones of beige and blue and red, colors taken from an Oriental rug that separated a small seating area from the rest of the store.

Diamond jewelry in gold settings was displayed on a background of deep royal-blue velvet. Other pieces in white gold, or perhaps platinum, were on red velvet. In one case, hundreds of loose gems were artfully arranged like a river of ice cascading over the landscape of velvet.

Everywhere she looked, Sara saw elegance—in paintings on the walls, in rich drapes at the windows, even the gate barring entrance into a back room was made of delicately scrolled wrought-iron that looked like a work of art. Classical music played softly through unseen speakers.

It was all so understated in a rich and sumptuous way.

This was what the Parks family had. This was what their children believed to be their birthright. But part of this empire should have belonged to *her* family. And what of Tyler and Conrad, Walter Parks's sons through his affair with their mother?

The door swung open, interrupting her inspection.

A subtle tension entered the elegant showroom. The woman in black straightened slightly, as if coming to attention. A younger man, busy shining an already shiny counter, became busier. Three elderly women, who had been discussing a graduation present for their niece, glanced up, then smiled at the man who'd entered.

Sara recognized him at once.

Walter Parks was sixty, but he was a man who kept himself in good physical shape. He was trim and athletic-looking, his face deeply tanned and leathery from hours in the sun. Tennis, she thought. Golf. Exclusive country clubs. He could afford the membership and greens fees.

At six-two, he was as tall as his son and her neighbor, Cade. His hair was salt-and-pepper gray, his eyes brown.

She hated him on sight.

Rachel laid a hand on her arm and gestured toward the man as he walked through the store and went behind the far counter. Sara nodded that she knew who he was.

"Did the courier arrive?" he asked the store manager, not bothering with a greeting.

"Yes. I put the package in the safe."

He nodded and disappeared into the back.

Murderer. Murderer. Murderer.

The word pounded in Sara's head with each beat of her heart. She could hear her mother's weakened voice, murmuring his name and the accusation as she sank into a coma, her heart giving up the battle to sustain life.

"Make…him…pay," Marla had whispered to her children as they gathered at her bedside.

"We will," Tyler had vowed.

"Let's go," Sara said to Rachel. "Let's get out of here."

After one glance at Sara, Rachel nodded and took her arm, leading her outside and away from the sight of anyone in the store. Sara leaned against the building and forced air into her constricted lungs.

"Are you all right?" Rachel asked.

"Yes. I think so," Sara added, pushing a smile onto her face. "I am. Really."

"I didn't think about him walking in the door while we were there," Rachel admitted. "It took us both by surprise."

"Yes. He looks like…"

"Cade?" Rachel guessed.

Sara nodded. "I didn't realize there would be so much family resemblance." She shook her head slightly as if to ward off the comparison. "I think I'm ready to go home."

Back at Sara's house, Rachel dropped her off, then rolled down the car window. "Don't forget our big date tomorrow night," she called out, laughter in her voice.

"I won't." Sara waved goodbye before opening the door to her place. No one seemed to be in next door.

Thinking of Stacy, she was filled with regret for the future and the possible hurt to the girl and her father. But then, there was all the regret of the past that Marla Carlton and her four children had had to live with.

"You're all dressed up," Stacy said Saturday evening, coming out the door and sitting on the stoop beside Sara.

Sara wore a red knit pantsuit that was one of her favorite outfits and a splurge last year when she'd been happy. Before her fiancé, Chad, then her mother, had died.

"I'm going out to dinner with my brother and his friend tonight. Miss Hanson is going, too."

Stacy nodded as if she approved.

Sara glanced up and down the street. "She's supposed to be here by now, but she's late."

"Maybe she had a wreck like my mother did."

The child's matter-of-fact suggestion startled Sara. Stacy's world had been shaken by her mother's death when she was three. Sara wondered again how much the child remembered. Did the bright youngster recall anything her grandfather and father might have said—

Realizing where this thought was leading, Sara broke it off, appalled at the idea of quizzing a child about her family's private conversations. She could never be a detective as Tyler was, asking intrusive questions and suspecting people of lies and evasions.

"Hello," a masculine voice said behind them.

Sara stood, her gaze held by Cade's as he stepped out the door. His smile was warm and beguiling, but in an open way, as if his thoughts were as innocent as his daughter's.

Since meeting this man, she'd realized how self-centered her fiancé had been. He'd always insisted on having his way. Cade was considerate and good-natured.

"Good evening," she said, sounding breathless and

unsure of herself as undefined emotion clutched at her throat, making it difficult to breathe.

"You look especially lovely tonight."

"She's waiting for her boyfriend," Stacy informed him.

Sara felt heat rise to her face. "Just friends," she quickly corrected. "And my brother."

Two cars arrived at the same time. Rachel pulled into the driveway behind Sara's car. Tyler stopped at the curb and got out. "Ready?" he asked, coming up the sidewalk.

"Yes," Sara answered.

She realized she had to introduce the two men. She did so quickly. Tension crawled along her nerves like a poisonous snake as the men shook hands and spoke.

"You look like Sara," Stacy said.

Tyler dropped to his haunches and shook her hand as Sara introduced the child. "Yes, all of the kids in my family look like our mother."

"I look like my daddy," Stacy told him.

Tyler studied her, then her father. "You sure do," he agreed. He smiled at the child, then stood. "We have dinner reservations, so we'd better get along."

"Have a pleasant evening," Cade said.

Rachel was already seated in the back of Tyler's car along with Nick Banning, Sara noted when she and Tyler joined them. She sat in the front passenger seat.

"I recognized Cade Parks," Nick said when they

were on their way. "The child was his daughter, I presume?"

"Yes. Stacy. She'll be in my class Monday."

"I don't think I'm ready to face a roomful of rowdy kids." Rachel made a fearful grimace.

Nick chuckled, then became serious. "Mark is meeting us at the restaurant."

"Has he learned anything?" Tyler demanded.

"I don't know. He'll tell us when he sees us."

At the cozy Italian restaurant, complete with an accordion player, the two couples met Nick's older brother.

"My brother, Mark," Nick introduced them. "He's a private detective and is helping us on the case."

Mark Banning wasn't old—early thirties, perhaps—but his eyes said he'd seen enough to last a lifetime. A terrible scar under his right eye spoke of his days with the New York police force, before he and Nick had moved to San Francisco and he'd opened his own detective agency.

Sara took Mark's hand. Smiling into his eyes, she said, "Thank you for helping us."

His manner was introspective and serious. "I believe in justice being done."

After they were seated, she leaned close to him. "Have you found anything on Derek Ross?"

"Yes. At least, I think I have. Tyler mentioned your mother once said her brother was a book lover and collected antique volumes."

Sara nodded. "Yes, she did." She waited impatiently as they placed their orders with the waiter. "You've traced him?" she asked as soon as they were alone again.

"Not quite, but I did some checking with a dealer in rare books who I ran into while investigating a theft once." Mark paused while he studied first Tyler, then Sara. "I asked him if he'd heard of Derek Ross. He hadn't, but he had done business over the years with a man called Derek Moss."

"Oh," Sara said in disappointment.

"Lots of times, when people change their names, they use the same initials…or something very similar to their real names, usually by changing one or two letters."

"You think…" she began, then stopped, almost afraid to voice the question.

Mark shrugged. "I've got a trace going on the man. The dealer couldn't find an address in his records, but he's pretty sure Derek Moss has, or had, a bookstore. Moss got a discount on the books due to having a retailer's license."

Sara's mind whirled with the possibility of finishing the case so soon. She pictured the tall, older man she'd seen in the jewelry store behind bars, paying for his crimes against her family.

Tyler must have had the same thought. "It's odd," he said, "to discover that you belong to another family, that your father is a man you despise, that you have other brothers and sisters you've never known.

And a five-year-old niece who's bright and friendly...
and innocent.''

At once another image imposed itself in her
mind—Cade Parks and Stacy, their eyes accusing as
they stared at her.

Pressing a hand to her chest, where a ball of pain
and misery formed, she wondered for the hundredth
time that week if she and Tyler were doing the right
thing. People were going to be hurt....

''You and Rachel might have an additional
worry,'' Mark told them. ''Cade Parks is on the board
of directors at your school. Cause trouble for his family and he could get you fired.''

Chapter Four

Walter Parks paced the floor in quick, furious strides on Monday morning. Someone was checking into his life, both personal and business, and he didn't like it, not one bit.

Get rid of one problem, it seemed, and two appeared. That was certainly the case in the present situation. Marla was dead, but her brats weren't.

Just to be sure the past stayed in the past, he'd had the detective check on them. One, a rather well-known mystery writer, had moved from Denver to New York. One of the twin boys had stayed in Colorado. So far, so good.

He paced some more as rage rose to a choking level inside him. He wanted to punch somebody. He wanted to rip something to shreds, to destroy the things that stood in the way of his complete freedom and relief from worry.

Like the two Carltons who now lived in San Francisco.

Dammit, twenty-five years was long enough to suffer for a moment of madness. He'd paid for it. He'd spent his life always having to watch over his shoulder, wondering if Marla would speak up—

"Mr. Parks, Cade is here," his secretary interrupted his pacing with the announcement.

He glanced toward the open door. Connie was forty-three, a single mother with a gifted son who attended the university at Berkeley, thanks to him. She'd worked for him for fifteen years. He provided her with a good living and a few other perks. In return, she was a totally reliable secretary and a discreet mistress.

Why couldn't all of life be as simple?

"Tell him to come in," Walter said impatiently. "Close the door," he said to his son as soon as Cade was inside.

A fleeting expression of annoyance crossed the boy's face. Well, he could just be annoyed. Walter was furious.

"Do you know who lives next door to you?" Walter demanded as soon as they were alone.

Cade was surprised by the question. "Yes, Sara Carlton," he admitted warily. Knowing his father, he felt there was more to the question than paternal curiosity.

"Yes. Sara Carlton," Walter repeated in a nasty tone.

Cade waited until the irritation settled before he asked, "What about her?"

His father paced the room like an angry lion, caged and resenting it, ready to lash out at anyone who got in his way. Cade was familiar with Walter's temper. Usually he waited it out without saying much. At the moment, he didn't like either his father's attitude or the subject.

"Do you also know her brother is a detective on the police force here?"

Cade nodded.

"And you never thought to mention it to me?"

"No. Why should I?"

"Someone has been making inquiries about… about the family business," Walter announced, his face becoming red as his anger rose higher. A vein throbbed in his neck.

Cade noted the hesitation and knew his father had changed what he'd been about to say. Lately, in dealing with the family patriarch, he'd had uneasy hunches that all was not well. His father's mood swings had grown increasingly unpredictable.

"How do you know?" Cade asked.

His father paused again, as if deciding on how much to tell him. "Someone claiming to be with the IRS called the bank and asked about the company's accounts and my personal ones. When I called the local IRS chief, he indicated they were looking into certain matters on companies dealing with imported diamonds. He wouldn't say why.''

"There could be lots of reasons—money laundering or gem smuggling from countries engaged in war. The press calls them 'conflict diamonds.'" Cade shrugged. "Since we don't do business with those countries or with smugglers, and the taxes are in order, we don't have anything to worry about.''

Walter stopped pacing and spun around. "A man in my position always has to worry.''

"Why?'' Cade asked, keeping his tone neutral.

His father glared at him so hotly, Cade wouldn't have been surprised if a laser beam burned right through his forehead.

"People are envious of those who pull themselves up and make it in life.''

By marrying into the business, Cade thought but didn't voice the accusation. For a second, he felt the overwhelming loss of his mother. Like Sara, his world had changed when he was four. He'd never understood why she had to be sent away.

When asked, his father had sorrowfully admitted that Anna Parks was "unstable'' and couldn't be trusted outside the mental hospital, that she was in the most progressive sanitarium in the world and, if she could be helped, the doctors there were the ones to do it. All he would tell the children was that Anna was safe and happy, insofar as she could be, and living in Switzerland.

Seeing his father's agitation, Cade tried to figure out what the old man was getting at. "So, is someone threatening you in some way? Did you get a poison pen letter or a call or something like that?"

"No," Walter snapped. "But I don't trust the Carlton brother and sister. They're here to make trouble."

"What kind of trouble?" Knowing Sara and having met her brother, Cade couldn't bring himself to take his father's odd worries seriously.

"Their father..."

Again the odd hesitation, Cade noted.

"Jeremy Carlton and I were partners on a project long ago," Walter said, his eyes narrowed as if he saw directly into the past. "Things were going bad for him, but I didn't know he was in financial trouble. Anyway, there was a rumor about smuggled diamonds, but I never paid it much attention. When Jeremy drowned—"

"Aboard a yacht our company owned at the time," Cade interrupted. "I was curious and checked into it after Sara moved in next door," he said when his father gave him a questioning glare.

"Yes," Walter said. "He drowned and that was the end of it. His family apparently lost everything. They moved to Colorado and I lost track of them after that."

"I see," Cade murmured. "What kind of project were you and Carlton working on?"

Walter's strained features relaxed somewhat. "We were going to produce the most expensive diamond necklace in the world, using nothing but the rarest of flawless stones. That was to be our launch into the market for the ultrarich."

"Celebrity chasing," Cade murmured, a degree of scorn showing through.

"Not celebrities. The truly rich," his father asserted, "are those who can afford a string of polo ponies, who have their own planes and seagoing yachts. Their net worth is over half a billion, and they take pains to stay out of the public eye."

"A very small market base."

"In that price range, we wouldn't have needed many sales to ensure our fortune."

A chill crept along Cade's nape at his father's smile. Cold, greedy and calculating wouldn't begin to describe it. "The company has done just fine over the years."

"We're overextended," Walter stated flatly.

"The economy has slowed down some, but the rich are with us always. And they always want something bigger and better than their neighbors."

"In business, a man can never relax. I want you to have the Carlton girl fired."

"What?" Cade wasn't sure he'd heard right.

"You're on the board of directors at the school. Get rid of her. Make sure she has to move, too. You have the phone number where the artist can be reached, don't you? Tell him she's throwing wild parties or something.''

"I'll do no such thing," Cade informed his father, his own anger building at his father's scheming.

Walter placed both hands on his desk and leaned closer, his eyes boring into Cade's. "You will if you want to keep that ranch you're so crazy about. I got you your position with the law firm. I can take it away."

Cade took a deep breath. Another one. It was no use. He headed for the door.

"Where the hell are you going? I'm not through talking to you," his father said in a snarl.

"I'm leaving," Cade said, keeping his own tone quiet and carefully controlled. "Before I punch you out. It's never good form to beat up one's father."

He walked out without looking back. The secretary kept her gaze pinned to the papers on her desk as he swept past.

Cade was careful around her. He and his siblings had figured out long ago that anything they said to her would be repeated to their father.

In the hall, he nearly ran over Linda Mailer, his father's accountant. "Sorry," he muttered.

"It was my fault," she said. "I wasn't watching where I was going." She gestured at the sheaf of papers in her hand. "Do you have a moment? I have some questions—"

"Later," Cade said and forced a smile. "I have to be somewhere."

Anywhere but in the vicinity of his father, Cade thought, going outside and breathing deeply.

The day was clear and warm, an invitation to be outside in the summer sun. Perusing the display of jewelry in the store window, he experienced an overpowering need to get away from everything that bore his father's touch. The ranch was just the place for that.

"It's no problem," Sara assured Tai Monday afternoon. She'd agreed to take Stacy home and let the child stay with her until Cade arrived.

"Thanks, Sara. That's a load off my mind," Tai said, relief mingling with the worry in her eyes.

The young woman's mother had undergone emergency surgery during the night for a ruptured appendix. Tai, an only child, needed to take care of her for a few days until the older woman was on her feet again.

"Don't worry about a thing. I'll explain what happened to Cade." Sara walked the premed student to the classroom door and waved as Tai hurried from the school grounds.

It was lunch recess and the babble of conversation and laughter on the playground was reassuring to Sara. As long as there were children and laughter, then the world couldn't be all bad.

But it could be harsh.

She thought of Tai's concern for her mom, of the past winter and her own mother's slow fading, those thin hands growing paler and colder each day as Marla's heart failed in its effort to supply the vital link to life.

With the death of her mother, Sara had felt adrift in life, cut off from her roots and all the past generations that made her the person she was. The future had seemed dark and fuzzy, an endless road leading to a place she couldn't see. Sensing Tai's fear had revived her own.

The bell rang, signaling the end of the lunch period. The children ran about in seeming disorder, but soon sorted themselves into lines in front of their classrooms, then marched in with their teachers.

Sara put the past out of her mind and finished her teaching duties. She ended the day by having the children dance around the classroom in time to a lively tune, then she and the twenty students straightened up the room in preparation for the next day.

"Stacy, you'll walk home with me," she told the youngster when the final bell rang. "Tai's mom got sick and Tai will have to stay with her for a couple of weeks."

Stacy smiled happily. "I like being with you. And Tai," she added, loyal to her sitter.

"You're a very likable person to be with, too," Sara said. "Shall we plan dinner for your father tonight since Tai won't be there to start it?"

"Let's have spaghetti. That's his favorite food."

Sara gave a little skeptical snort. "I think I know

whose favorite it is,'' she said as Stacy skipped along beside her.

Stacy pressed a hand over her mouth and giggled.

At the town house, they worked together and soon the spicy sauce was bubbling in the pan. While it simmered, the two weeded the front flower beds, not that they needed much work. The mysterious Mr. Lee—Sara had never seen him—kept the grounds in tip-top shape.

That's where Cade found them when he arrived at six o'clock.

After the usual hug, swing and nose-rubbing with his daughter, he turned to Sara. His stare was so intent, she became flustered and dropped the small bunch of grass sprouts they'd pulled from among the flowers.

''We cooked dinner,'' Stacy told him.

''Where's Tai?'' he asked Sara.

''Her mommy's sick,'' Stacy answered. ''Tai has to stay with her 'cause she had a op'ration.''

''*An* operation,'' he corrected.

''Mommy wanted Daddy to have one, but he got mad,'' Stacy said to Sara. The child gazed earnestly at her father. ''Sara and I could stay with you if you had one,'' she volunteered.

Before Sara could quite figure out the implications, Cade abruptly set the girl on her feet, unlocked the door and disappeared inside with her. His face had turned an interesting shade of red.

Sara felt her own face heat up as she sorted through

the conversation. While working together last week, Rachel had told Sara all she'd read about Cade's wife. The woman had been an ardent partygoer. It didn't take a strong leap to imagine her not wanting more children...or that she'd wanted Cade to do something about it.

Had he?

Going inside, she prepared the pasta and salad and rolls, then studied the ebony table with its perfect finish. She'd never used it.

Getting a colorful tablecloth from her belongings, she went onto the deck and spread it over the patio table there. With the table set and the food ready to bring out, she wondered what to do next.

Feeling embarrassed and more than a little foolish, she knocked on Cade's back door.

He answered in less than a minute. He'd changed to jeans and a blue chambray shirt, the sleeves rolled up and the buttons not yet fastened down the front.

His chest was lightly sprinkled with dark hair. His skin was tanned. She wondered when he spent time outside to acquire it. He wasn't a brawny man, but he looked strong and fit, with a whipcord leanness to him that spoke of latent energy, ready to be unleashed on a second's notice.

Unexpected hunger uncoiled and flooded her with intense longing. She hadn't felt passion in so long it took a moment to realize fully what it was.

She wanted this man. She wanted his arms around her. She wanted to feel his warmth, his intimate touch. She wanted to caress him, to explore his masculine flesh with her hands...with her body...

"Yes?" he said.

Sara hesitated at his tone—not exactly cold, but not exactly friendly, either. "Uh, did Stacy tell you we prepared dinner?"

"Yes. I was just about to call and see if the invitation was still open."

"Of course." She dredged up a smile. "I don't want to eat leftover spaghetti for the next six nights."

His answering smile was forced. "I'll get Stace. We'll be over in a minute."

"I, uh, thought we would eat on the deck."

"Great. We'll be right out."

Sara retreated, leaving her door open so they could come inside if they wished. Her fingers trembled slightly as she removed crisp sourdough bread from the oven and placed it in a cloth-lined basket. She made a nest for the sauce in the center of the pasta, which she'd placed on a platter with a high rim.

"I'll take that," Cade said, coming to the door. He removed the platter from her hand.

"Thanks. Stace, if you'll put these rolls on the table, I'll get drinks. Milk or iced tea?"

"Tea for me, milk for the young lady," Cade said.

Since it was early, the air hadn't cooled to the point of being chilly. The temperature was a pleasant seventy-two degrees. With the irrepressible Stacy there to bridge any awkward pauses, the tension between

Sara and Cade eased and the evening became quite cheerful.

"So, did both of you enjoy your first day of school?" he asked when they were seated.

The two females gave him a thorough review of their day while the shadows lengthened and the sun hid behind the fog bank on the horizon. They finished the meal, but lingered at the table and talked.

"There'll be no flash tonight," Cade told them, gazing at the horizon.

Sara thought he looked wistful, but in the next instant, as his eyes met hers, she decided she was wrong. She'd been aware of his gaze on her several times during the meal, but his thoughts had been too obscure to read. Now he merely looked amused and somehow distant.

Not that they'd ever been close, except as children in school together, she mused, her senses keenly aware of him and his physical presence, the innate masculinity that called to something equally strong but feminine in her.

After eating, they all pitched in to clean up the dishes, then Cade and Stacy went to their place so the child could get ready for bed. Sara draped a sweater over her shoulders and returned to the deck.

Twilight deepened into night, and still she lingered. No mosquitoes came out to annoy her. Few sounds from the street penetrated back here. It didn't even feel as if she were in a city.

"Would you like a glass of wine?" Cade asked from his doorway an hour later.

"Yes, that would be nice."

He joined her on the deck and handed her a glass of wine, which was red and mellow, holding only a hint of tannin from the oak barrel in which it had been aged.

"Very good," she murmured after taking a sip.

"An eight-year-old Cabernet," he told her. "It won the blue ribbon in a recent international competition."

"You should have saved it for a special occasion."

"I think this is special enough. A fine dinner and interesting conversation, two beautiful women to share the evening—what more could a man want?"

The cheer sounded somewhat forced, but his voice had deepened. It flowed over her with the same dark complexities as the wine, a subtle weaving of spicy flavors that spoke of other pleasures to come—

She stopped the train of thought with an effort. She couldn't afford to think like that. Rising, she stood by the railing and stared out toward the sea.

Ships were visible as lights that rose and dipped with the movement of the sea. They struck her as unbearably lonely as they sailed off into the night.

But she knew the loneliness was in herself. She swallowed the painful knot in her throat when Cade came over and stood beside her.

"I used to watch the ships when I was a kid," he said. "I wanted to go on a grand adventure with the sailors, a modern-day Jason on the trail of the golden fleece.''

She heard and understood the undertone of sadness when he chuckled at his boyish ideas. It reached down into her own heart and opened places she'd thought were closed forever.

"We all have dreams," she said in hardly more than a whisper. "And we all have to grow up."

"Some more quickly than others. You, I think."

"And you," she murmured.

"Perhaps," he said.

She knew a lot about his life now and wondered if he was thinking of his mother, who'd been sent away to a very private hospital, it was rumored, for the mentally ill. Mark Banning had told them this news.

"When your mother was sent away?" she asked.

He was silent for a long moment. "Yes. It was like the sun went out."

His voice was so low she had to strain to hear. "Do…do you ever see her?"

"No. My father thinks it would serve no purpose. She has the best of care and, according to him, she wouldn't be interested in any of her children anyway."

"I'm sorry." She couldn't deny the compassion she felt for him and his loss.

"Into every life…" He shrugged philosophically.

"Some rain must fall," she finished when he stopped.

His smile appeared, a beacon in the dark. "We're getting awfully serious, young Sara."

"I don't feel young. I haven't for a long time."

He touched her shoulder. Warmth flowed from his hand all the way to the center of her. Without meaning to, she leaned into him when he stepped closer. He slipped both arms around her, clasping his hands over her tummy and tucking her against his body.

For some reason, it made her ache inside, as if her heart were weeping. She laid her hands over his. They stayed that way for a long time, not speaking as they watched a few stars appear.

"Without the glare of city lights," he said, "you can see a million stars. At the ranch, the only way to tell the ocean from the night sky is to note where the stars begin."

"You have a ranch?"

"Yes. I plan to go up Friday night. Stace and I would like to have you join us."

"I may have work to do," she hedged, wanting to go but not sure if she should. When she glanced up, he lowered his head and gently touched her lips with his.

"Sara," he said, his voice soft, husky.

A tremor rushed over her. He tightened his hold, then stepped to the side, turning her at the same time. They faced each other, their expressions solemn, their eyes questioning. She wondered if his doubts were the same as hers. At the moment, it didn't matter.

Slowly she raised her hands and caressed along his shirtfront. "Warm, so warm," she said.

"Burning up," he admitted.

Cade cupped her face in his hands and sipped from her lips as if he'd found a rare and perfect wine, a nectar of incredible sweetness stolen from the gods. And like all mortals who dared the fates, he knew he would pay…someday…somehow….

He groaned as need pushed aside the dire musing. He took her mouth in a kiss of fire, of insatiable passion. He needed more from her.

"Have to touch you," he said in half apology, half anticipation.

"Yes. Oh, yes." Sara wanted nothing between them—no clothing, no second thoughts, no past filled with hatred and regret. She pushed her hands under his shirt and caressed his back.

The muscles flexed beneath her fingers, hinting at raw power kept under tight control. She wanted to experience that power for herself, to feel it against her…in her.

She turned her head and sighed shakily. "This is…we shouldn't… It's so…unwise."

"I know," he whispered, his mouth hot on her neck just below her ear. "Stop me. If you can." Cade chuckled ruefully, knowing she was as caught up in the moment as he was. Something primitive and wild flashed through his blood, driving out sanity in the face of this terrible need. For her. For this woman.

"Come. We need to go inside," he said, feeling

her tremble again. He held his breath as he turned them toward her door.

"Stacy," she said.

"I have the monitor on. With the doors open, we'll hear if she calls out." He guided her inside.

Sara felt the sofa touch the back of her knees. She tossed the sweater on a chair and kicked off her shoes when Cade did. He enclosed her in a warm embrace and together they sank onto the cushions.

Their bodies meshed as if they'd done this a thousand times. They stretched out on the supple leather—thighs locked, chests and abdomens touching, hands reaching, searching beneath the barriers of their clothing until they could touch living flesh.

"Your skin is as smooth as flower petals," he murmured as he imprinted kisses over her face.

"So is yours," she said just as ardently, completely entranced by the growing intimacy.

His low laughter delighted her, and she laughed, too. It felt natural and reassuring.

"I need more," he said.

She let him unfasten the buttons on her blouse, helped shed it and the bra, then waited, her heart surging like a storm-driven tide, as he unfastened his shirt and wrapped her in it so that skin nestled against skin.

"You're burning me up," he told her, his mouth stirring her to madness as he kissed along her neck, then drew back enough to lave her peaked breasts with his tongue until she gasped and moaned with hunger.

Arching slightly, she moved against him, feeling the enticing hardness against her tummy. He clasped her thigh in one hand and positioned it over his hip.

"Oh," she cried softly as sensation whirled through her at the greater contact. She only had to press slightly to experience even more.

He moved with her, their breathing shallow and rapid as the flames danced and leaped through their entwined bodies.

"Cade," she whispered. "You must…you must come to me…."

"I want to," he assured her. "But I didn't expect this. I didn't prepare for it." He caught her hand when she tugged at his jeans, then pressed her palm against his chest. "No more. I don't have protection."

She bit into her bottom lip as disappointment hit. "You, uh, the operation…"

"A vasectomy was Rita's idea. I never had one." He gazed into her eyes. "Unless you're protected, we have to stop…now."

A tangle of questions wrapped around them, buzzed like angry bees between them as they contemplated each other solemnly. His smile was unexpected—a rueful acknowledgment of their predicament.

"Okay, let's quit while we're ahead," he said.

He swung up and away from her. The night air from the open door swept over her, chilling the ardor to embers but not quite putting the fire out. She sighed.

''Me, too,'' he said. He leaned down and kissed her lightly, picked up his shoes and departed.

Sara wrapped her sweater around her shivering body. Sitting there in the dark, she went over the events of the evening. There had been such strange undercurrents between them. And then the passion.

She'd never known a man like Cade. Gentle. Caring. A wonderful father. There was something deeply honorable about him. She felt it in her bones. She should tell him why she'd come to San Francisco. Before he found out in a different way. Like when the police came to arrest his father.

''Complexities,'' she said aloud and sighed again.

Chapter Five

Two nights later, the ring of the doorbell startled Sara as she sat in the den and tried to read a long novel about a rich family and their problems.

She personally thought it would do the fictional characters good to take on a poor family's problems and see how life felt when there wasn't enough money to buy one's way out of difficulty.

Rising, she went to the front door. It was too late for Stacy to be up and she assumed Cade would use the back door since the den was in the rear of the house. That left Tyler to be calling at nine-thirty in the evening.

She was right. Flicking off the dead bolt, she opened the elegant portal and invited him in. "Did you just get off work?" she asked, seeing his suit.

"Yeah." He rubbed a hand over his face after entering the town house. "Got anything to eat?"

"Ham-and-cheese sandwich or omelette?"

"Omelette. Three eggs. I'm starved."

After locking the door, she led the way into the kitchen. "Don't they let police detectives eat in this city?" she asked with a sympathetic glance.

"Not if they can help it." His smile was weary.

She prepared a large omelette and poured it into a skillet. While it cooked, she dropped an English muffin into the toaster, considered, then added one for herself. In a few minutes, she handed Tyler a tray with his food and carried one for herself with the toasted muffin, strawberry jam and a glass of milk on it.

They ate in the den with the trays across their laps. "So what's happening?" she demanded when her brother remained stubbornly silent.

He roused from his introspection. "Trouble."

The hair prickled on the back of her neck. "What kind of trouble?"

He shrugged. "Don't know." He finished off the omelette and the last drink of milk. "Got any coffee?"

"I'll make you a latte." She prepared the steamed milk and coffee, did one for herself, then returned. "Help yourself," she said dryly, noting that he had devoured the other half of her muffin and jam and was swallowing the last of her milk.

"Sorry. I was still hungry."

She handed him the steaming mug and settled onto the sofa again. "Has Mark Banning found our dear uncle?"

Tyler shook his head. "Someone tried to hack into my computer, though, and set up a worm to send everything I had on file to a third computer."

Alarm spread through Sara. "Who?"

"I couldn't trace 'em. They covered their tracks well."

"Did they find out anything about our quest?"

"No. Fortunately I use a separate drive for all Internet searches and then check it for viruses and worms after each session on the Net. That's when I discovered someone was trying to implant a tracking program on me."

"We haven't tried to hide," she reminded him. "We use our real names. Do you think Walter Parks had anything to do with the hacker?"

"Why do you ask?"

"Well, I live next door to his son. Cade remembers me from years ago. If he mentioned me to his father, then Walter would know the Carltons—at least some of us—are back in town."

"And he might wonder exactly what we're doing here," Tyler concluded.

"Only if he has a guilty conscience. Otherwise why would he care?"

Her brother snorted. "I've done some research on his business dealings. He's known to be a ruthless competitor. I doubt his conscience bothers him much.''

''Cade doesn't seem at all like his father,'' she murmured, recalling the son's determination to be a better parent to his daughter than his father had been to him and his siblings.

''Have you found out anything from him?'' Tyler asked.

''Like what?''

''How the family business is prospering? The old man has been doing a lot of buying lately. There's been a large payment to a foreign diamond dealer of dubious reputation through an overseas bank. There's also been a couple of mysterious deliveries to his store of late. Uninsured deliveries by courier.''

''So?''

Her brother shrugged. ''So, I don't know. Too bad the company is family-owned. Their records are private, so it's more difficult to check on their business dealings. But not impossible,'' he added. ''Twenty-five years ago, the Parks empire seemed to take off. Where did the money come from?''

''The Carlton diamond business that apparently somehow disappeared into thin air without a trace just as Father did during that ill-fated yachting party?''

''That's what I think,'' her brother confirmed her guess.

Sara sipped the latte while she thought. ''You and Nick and Mark Banning have the inside track on the investigation. I feel rather useless in the grand scheme of things. What do you want me to do?''

''Feed me when I drop by?'' Tyler suggested with a grin, then became serious again. ''The son knows the business. Can you get him to talk about the family's fortunes? See if he knows how much was inherited from his mother's side of the family. Walter Parks didn't have much but ambition and a sharp mind before he married. As soon as his father-in-law died, two years after the marriage, Walter changed the name of the company from Lindsay Mining to Parks Mining and Exploration.''

Sara glanced at her brother in surprise at this news. ''You have been busy. There's something that occurs to me as sort of suspicious. Remember Mark told us that shortly after the party on the yacht, Walter sent his wife to a Swiss sanitarium?''

''Swiss, huh? I don't think Mark knows that. I'll have him start checking—''

''Sorry, that was just a manner of speaking. In novels, people always get sent to reclusive Swiss hospitals high in the mountains when their kin want to get rid of them. Anyway, Anna Parks was sent overseas somewhere when Cade was a child. He said the children never saw her, that his father said she wouldn't care about them.''

''So?''

Sara frowned intently into the middle distance while she marshaled her thoughts. ''Don't you think that's rather convenient and coincidental? According to Mother, Anna was present at the celebration aboard the yacht. What if she saw her husband have a quarrel with his partner? Maybe they got into a fight and our father, sorry, my father—''

''It's okay. I still think of Jeremy Carlton as my father, too,'' Tyler assured her.

''So maybe Jeremy fell and broke his neck or something. Then Walter panicked and threw the body overboard and Anna witnessed the whole thing. If she insisted her husband go to the police with the truth, then he might have needed to shut her up. What better way than to get her committed to an asylum for the insane in a foreign country?''

''Good point,'' Tyler murmured.

''Also,'' Sara continued. ''When did he go into the retail business? It seems to me it would take a lot of money to open a jewelry store, and now he owns two of the most prestigious ones in California. Was that after our family somehow lost everything?''

Tyler ground the heels of his hands into his eye sockets as if he could erase the weariness. He covered a huge yawn before answering. ''He has a way of taking over any enterprise he's involved in while his partners—I use that term loosely—have a way of losing out.''

''Or disappearing,'' Sara reminded him. ''Tyler, be careful. I feel threatened. I don't know if that's the right word, but I have this odd feeling, like a noose tightening around us. Both of us.''

He patted her arm as he rose. ''I always pay attention to hunches and odd feelings. I think we're making someone nervous—''

"Walter Parks," she said grimly, also standing and walking toward the front to see him out.

"Yeah. Are you going to back out?"

"No. Why would you think that?"

"Just a feeling." He gave her an insouciant grin, then nodded his head toward the other town house. "He was pretty interested to see who rode up front with me and who rode in the back with Nick when we went to dinner Saturday night. Anything going on between you two that I should know about?"

Sara sighed and wrinkled her nose at her smart-mouthed sibling. "He's very attractive," she finally admitted.

"Aha," Tyler said softly as they arrived at the front door and paused there.

"It's confusing. He doesn't seem ruthless. In fact, he's a wonderful father."

"Even an animal looks after its own."

"I know. He's my enemy and yet..." She shrugged.

Tyler studied her for a few seconds, then rubbed his brow as if his head hurt. "Sometimes lightning strikes, and there you are, burned to the core."

The words were so startling, so much like a confession, that Sara was startled. "Tyler, have you met someone? Are you in love?"

His brief laughter was tinged with bitterness. "Hardly. It was nothing. A one-night stand."

Sara was confused. "But if there're feelings—"

"Forget it," he said. "The lady obviously did."

With very mixed emotions, Sara studied him. Tyler—who'd vowed he would never marry or have kids and "all that stuff" as he used to scornfully mutter—in love?

Well, maybe not in love, but certainly a chord had been struck in him by someone. Unfortunately, it appeared the same thing hadn't struck her.

"Wait," she requested when he opened the door. "Cade has invited me out to his ranch with him and Stacy this weekend. I told him I might be busy."

"Go," Tyler said at once. "This could be a chance to pry some info out of him. See if you can find out how the Parks empire is faring money-wise. Maybe he knows of some new deals his father is putting together. Or what was in those packages the courier dropped off."

"Right, like he's going to tell me they're smuggling diamonds or something."

Her brother gave her a sardonic glance. "Men have been known to disclose a lot during a weak moment."

Her face flushed hotly in a sudden surge of guilt and remembered passion. Tyler touched her cheek. "Perhaps you and he have already had that moment?"

She shook her head. "There is an attraction. That's what worries me. I want to believe that Cade is decent and honorable, then I think of his father and what

Mother told us. It gets me confused and angry and frustrated.''

Tyler nodded. ''I know the feeling. Maybe you'd better stay out of it, let me and Nick and Mark handle everything.''

Sara shook her head. ''I came here to help. I'll stick it out. And do my part.''

''No matter what it takes?'' he asked.

''No matter what it takes.''

They agreed to meet Monday and discuss the weekend, then said good-night. Sara locked the door and returned to the den. She cleaned up the dishes and went to bed, but not to sleep. Too many restless thoughts filled her head.

''Miss Carlton, guess what?'' Stacy demanded Friday morning when Sara stopped at the adjoining town house to pick up the youngster for the short walk to school.

''What?''

''Dad and I are going to the ranch tonight and you're invited!''

''Yes, your father kindly included me,'' Sara admitted. She'd been over and over all the arguments about why she should go, but her conscience had bothered her all week. It seemed underhanded to take advantage of Cade's and Stacy's trust in her. ''I don't think I should intrude on your private time.''

''Please, you have to come. You haven't seen my pony. She's so beautiful. She can do tricks, too.''

"I think you've taken Miss Carlton by surprise," Cade said, opening the door wider and handing his daughter a bright red lunchbox. "The invitation is still open. Can you join us?"

Sara tried to think of a plausible excuse to refuse, but some willful part of her urged her to accept. "You're spending the night?"

"Yes. We'll leave early Sunday afternoon. Stace and I have a family dinner at my father's Sunday night."

Stacy wrinkled her nose. "Do we hafta?"

"Yes," her father said firmly.

Stacy went back to the original question. "Can you come to the ranch? We got cows and everything. We can help milk."

"You have milk cows?" Sara asked, surprised.

"Actually I lease the operation. The farmer also takes care of our five horses and two dogs. The ranch is a two-hour drive north of the city. We would really like for you to join us, if you haven't made plans for the weekend."

"Uh, no—"

"Please come," Stacy urged.

"Yes, do," the father chimed in. "I would consider it a slight repayment for the help you've given me and Stace while Tai is unavailable."

This really was a chance to find out more about his family, she decided, then wondered if she was rationalizing her desire to go. "Okay. It sounds like fun."

"Yay, she's going. I told you she would." Stacy

twirled around in delight. "We're leaving right after school."

"You're quitting work early?" Sara asked.

"I thought we would try to beat the traffic, if that's possible."

His smile made Sara's heart do weird things— speed up, skip a couple of beats and generally act silly. "What clothing will I need?" she asked.

"Jeans. A jacket. Boots, if you have them, otherwise sneakers will do. Do you ride?"

"I've never been on a horse in my life." She opened her eyes wide and gave them a horrified grimace.

Stacy burst into giggles, which were underscored by his deeper chuckles. "It's easy," the girl assured her teacher.

On the way to school, Sara wondered just how easy the weekend would be.

"This is lovely," Sara murmured that afternoon after they'd left the city and its traffic behind.

Cade expertly followed the winding coast road north of San Francisco. Bay laurel grew profusely along narrow canyons that opened at frequent intervals to the side of the highway. On one curve, the road had recently been repaved.

"There was a landslide during the March rains," he told her. "They had to build a bridge-type understructure to make the repair. The highway department would like to close the road, I think, but people object. On nice weekends, this is a busy stretch.''

''It's very scenic,'' she said.

They left the highway and turned toward the west, passing through ranch land where cows grazed.

''This is it,'' Stacy said from the back seat. ''This is our ranch.''

Cade drove over a grate designed to prevent livestock from crossing it. Fences stretched to either side, but no gate barred the gravel road from access. Black-and-white cows stared at them with casual interest.

''These are the milk cows,'' Stacy told her.

Cade drove past a large barn. ''The milking parlor,'' he explained. ''It has the latest equipment.''

A neat white house was set back from the road. Cade nodded toward it. ''Roger and Candy Mendolson. They milk two hundred cows twice a day, every day of the year. No time off for good behavior. Fortunately they have help, so everyone gets a weekend off once a month.''

''Gracious,'' Sara said. ''Teachers complain about only getting a month off during the summer when we're on the all-year program.''

''Roger and Candy say they wouldn't have it any other way. Life in a town would drive them nuts.''

''I can identify with that,'' Sara muttered darkly, drawing a chuckle from him.

The road sloped upward, then dropped over the top of a hillock. In a secluded dip of land nestled another house, one made of fieldstone on the bottom third, then split logs on the rest. A quarter mile away, the land dropped over a cliff to a rock-strewn beach that stretched northward until it disappeared into the salty haze from the sea.

"This is incredibly lovely," she said. "The grass is green."

Cade pulled into a carport and turned off the engine. "We get condensation from the coastal fog. That's why the fields along the coast stay relatively green in the summer. The cows will graze on dried grass, too."

Cade helped the two females out, then unlocked the front door. Inside the cottage, Sara surveyed the open living area that flowed into a small but modern kitchen. A natural stone fireplace dominated the main wall. To the left of the fireplace was a set of steps to the second story.

"Your bedroom is back here." Cade, carrying her suitcase, led the way down a short corridor. "The bathroom is directly across the hall. Linen closet there." He indicated the doors to each, then entered the bedroom.

The furniture was made of pine and was simple in design. There was a double bed, a tall, narrow chest of drawers between two windows, a lamp and table next to the bed and a cane chair with a blue cushion beside the table.

"Here's the closet in case you need to hang anything." Cade opened a door to show her a space about eighteen inches wide with a shelf over a clothes rod.

He put her case on the floor between the bed and the closet. "We usually walk down to the beach first thing. Do you feel up to joining us or would you rather rest?"

"I'd like to go, too," Sara said.

"Bring a jacket. It might be windy."

After he left, Sara removed her pajamas and toiletry case, laid the pj's on the bed and took the case to the bathroom to freshen up. Upstairs she could hear Stacy calling to her father, but couldn't make out the words.

When she returned to the main area, she stood at the window and looked toward the ocean. It was more gray than blue. The horizon blended into a barely discernible line separating sea and sky. For some reason, the lovely vista seemed vast and lonely.

She smiled slightly, knowing the feeling was within herself. A nagging sense of deception hung over her spirits.

Stacy clambered down the stairs and dashed toward the door. "Come on, let's beat Daddy to the shore."

Sara followed her student out of the cottage and along a path that led down a rocky slope into a ravine cut by the periodic flow of a creek. From there, they walked out on the sandy shore cluttered with rocks and boulders of various sizes. A few pieces of driftwood littered the beach.

Cade caught up with them when they paused to remove their shoes and socks. He grinned and added his to the boulder where they left their things.

"We were here first, Daddy," Stacy cried and

raced into the shallow waves that crested on the beach.

Sara was in the water past her ankles before the sensation of pain registered in her brain. "Oh, it's cold," she complained, hopping from one foot to the other.

"Your feet will be numb in a minute," Cade assured her.

"Right," Sara agreed. "As soon as they turn to ice."

"Look, sea lions," Stacy called, pointing to a large rock in the water. "You can tell 'cause they have ears."

"Sea lions still have visible external ears," Cade explained. "Seals don't. That's how you tell them apart."

The animals snoozed in the setting sun. One scratched lazily with a flipper. From down the coast, Sara could hear a foghorn sounding a warning off a rocky promontory.

"Each foghorn has its own signal," Cade told her. "By timing the blasts and the silence between, sailors can tell which lighthouse they're passing, even if it's foggy. The same is true of the flashes of light."

"How interesting," Sara said, throwing off her qualms about being there. "I didn't know that."

Behind them, the excited barking of two dogs drew their attention. The animals rushed down the ravine.

"Teddy! Rufus!" Stacy clapped her hands and called the two pets to her. The dogs raced around the girl, jumping, barking and licking her face in delight. One dog had a rusty red coat.

"That's Rufus," Cade told her. "Teddy is the brown-and-white one. Stace thought he looked like her teddy bear."

Teddy had thick fur with splotches of brown and white, and patches around each eye. Sara thought he looked more like a panda.

"I told her she should have named him Panda," Cade said, echoing her impression.

Their eyes met, and they both smiled.

Warmth flowed over her, reminding her of the heat that flared between them when they had kissed. She stared at his mouth and wanted that fire again.

"Keep that up and I'll be forced to kiss you," he murmured, touching her lower lip with a fingertip.

"Come on," Stacy yelled, running along the breaking waves with the two dogs circling around her. "Let's explore the cave. This way."

Flustered, Sara hurried after the girl. Behind her, she heard Cade's chuckle and knew that he knew she was running from him, from herself, from the passion that rose too readily between them.

After exploring a shallow cave farther down the line of cliffs, they returned to the ravine to climb the path back to the cottage.

"I'm hungry," Stacy announced upon their return.

Inside the cabin, they made sandwiches from supplies that Cade had brought, ate at a round pine table, then continued their exploration of the ranch.

"We'll go for a ride in the morning," Cade promised his daughter when five horses rushed to the fence and stuck their heads over the top of the barbed wire.

Sara slipped her jacket on as the sun dipped into the ocean and out of sight.

"It gets cold along the coast at night," Cade commented as they ambled back to the house.

Sara nodded. "I read something about the tides along the coast. The current sweeps out of the north, flowing from Alaska, then southward down the continent's edge. I assume that's why it cools down so much at night."

"Right. The current churns up colder water from the depths of the sea, which produces an afternoon breeze off the ocean and brings in the coastal fog."

"I like to walk in the fog," Stacy told them. "It's creepy. You could fall off the cliff."

"Which is why we don't run when we can't see more than a few feet in front of our noses," Cade reminded the child.

She laughed and ran ahead with the two dogs.

Cade shook his head as he lightly clasped Sara's hand. "Tell me, teacher, how do you keep up with that kind of energy from twenty kids?"

"With great difficulty," Sara said.

They again smiled at each other. It was a moment to savor, she thought. A time out of time, separate from all the troubles that had been or were to come.

"Let's make brownies for a snack," Stacy suggested when they were back in the cottage.

"Good idea," Cade said.

"Can we have a fire?" the girl wanted to know.

"After we get the brownies in the oven."

They ate in front of the fire, then played Go Fish until it was time for Stacy to go to bed. Cade escorted the child upstairs while Sara sat on the sofa, relaxing in pleasant idleness.

The evening seemed like something in a play—the perfect family holiday…before the aliens landed or the body was found or some other tragedy befell the players in the scene.

She gazed into the fire as a shiver rushed over her. Someone was walking over her grave, as her mother would have said.

Hearing Cade's steps on the stairs, she carefully wiped all emotion from her face and waited, heart pounding. She wasn't sure what she was waiting for.

Chapter Six

Sara knew, when her eyes met Cade's, that she'd lied to herself about her reasons for coming to his ranch. It wasn't for fact-finding, but for herself and the hunger that refused to be suppressed any longer.

In the soft lamplight, his eyes were dark and mysterious. Alarm sizzled through her body, warning her against being foolish, but even that couldn't overcome the intense need that surged like a lava flow in her blood.

He sat on the sofa beside her and kicked off his shoes, then propped his feet on the rustic coffee table that looked as if it had been made from saplings with the bark whittled away. The latest fishing and hunting magazines were stacked on it. Older editions were piled in a bookcase along a side wall. A small television resided on a shelf.

The cabin had a welcoming feel. It seemed comforting to her. A warm, safe place, the way a home should be.

But it wasn't her home, she reminded herself.

"We don't get cable here," he said. "And I haven't bothered with a satellite dish. Stacy and I keep movies and video games on hand. You ever played Banjo-Kazooie?"

Sara shook her head.

"We'll have to try it. Tomorrow, maybe."

When she glanced his way, the expression in his eyes told her movies and games weren't uppermost in his mind. A sensation of anticipation, so strong it was painful, rolled over her.

He moved close, crowding her, but she didn't mind. "I didn't bring you here for this," he said in a low tone, "but now that you're here, I can't stop thinking about it. About us. About making love with you."

Sara sighed. "I know. I've argued with myself all week, going over the reasons I shouldn't come up here and why it's impossible for us to become involved."

"Why?" he asked, leaning close and sliding his fingers into her hair. "Why is it impossible?"

Why? Let me count the ways... "I'm Stacy's teacher, for one thing."

He nodded. "She's the most important element in

this triangle. I don't want her hurt by anything that happens between us. I think we can guard against that."

"We hardly know each other."

"Ah, but that's not true. We've known each other all our lives."

His quick smile was almost her undoing, but she held to her argument. "Not really. A year in the same kindergarten class doesn't qualify as a lifelong friendship."

"It counts for something," he murmured huskily. "If I remember correctly, the second week of school you announced that we were going to be married when we grew up. Since then, when the world has seemed a dark and uncaring place, I've remembered that somewhere out there was a beautiful woman who loved me."

His smile was so wonderful as he teased her, she could have cried. He caressed her scalp with his fingertips, making little round motions that soothed and excited her at the same time.

With a sigh, partly of defeat, partly of anticipation, she turned her face to his. Their lips were mere inches apart as they gazed into each other's eyes.

"You remember because you associate me with happier times in your life." She cradled his handsome face in her hands, returning the intensity of his stare with that of her own. "It's the same with me. But Cade, that was long ago. So many years have passed.

So many things have happened to each of us." She dropped her hands to his chest.

"Yes, but we have this moment. The fact that we've found each other again must mean something."

His eyes were sexy and compelling while he waited patiently for her agreement or rejection. Unlike her former fiancé, Cade didn't insist on having things his way. He treated her as an equal, one who had opinions and needs as strong as his. She could have loved him for that reason alone.

No, not love, she quickly corrected. She wasn't in love with anyone. But she was terribly attracted to this man.

Sex for enjoyment only, without love and commitment? a hesitant part of her questioned.

"You're doing an awful lot of thinking," he murmured, a smile playing across his lips.

She managed a laugh. "I know. My sister calls me Plato when I take a long time to decide something. My mother said we should ask ourselves if, a year from now, we would regret whatever we'd done. She said to let that be our guide."

"A wise woman."

"I think she learned from experience," Sara told him, a strum of returning sadness running through her like the plaintive moan of a bass viol, low and mournful.

She stared into his eyes, then closed hers tightly, wanting his touch with everything in her.

When he kissed her, she forgot the qualms about

sharing passion while planning his father's downfall. Raking her fingers into his hair, she responded to the kiss by pulling him closer.

Cade felt as if he held a magical goddess who could change her form at will, becoming earth or air or water as well as flame. Whatever she was, her essence burned brightly through him. It tugged him ever closer to the pit of self-deception he'd experienced once before, when he'd thought fascination and desire were everlasting love.

When she slipped her hands under his shirt so that she was touching his flesh, he knew he would sell his soul to whatever devil wanted it, if he could but have her to himself for this one night.

He planted kiss after kiss over her mouth, her eyes, her throat. When he bit lightly, she gasped, then gave him a playful pinch on his chest.

Going back to her mouth, he tasted the honey inside, then parried the delectable thrusts of her tongue as they staged a mock battle, each knowing there would be no losers in this skirmish.

Sara soon found kisses weren't enough. She kicked off her slippers and swung her legs up and around so they were resting across his lap. He pressed against her so that she half reclined in the cozy corner.

With his chest touching hers, she arched upward while exploring the muscles of his back. His skin was warm and smooth, inviting her to roam further. Their breaths mingled intimately as the embrace grew ever deeper.

"This isn't going to be enough," he said in a low growl, deserting her lips to nibble on her ear. "I need to touch you...all over."

"I need it, too," she whispered, frustrated with the clothing that interfered with sensuous stroking.

He lifted his head. "Your bedroom is close. It has a lock on the door."

She could have refused. She could have weighed the situation and wisely refrained from giving in to temptation. It hardly crossed her mind. "Let's go there."

He stood and pulled her to her feet, then carried her on the short trip to the guest room. Standing her by the bed, he turned on the lamp, then closed and locked the door.

When he returned to her, her knees went weak as he took in all of her, from her head to her toes, his gaze rampant with hunger. With casual movements, he began to undress. She did the same. He finished first and helped her.

"Your hands are cold," he said, catching them between his and pressing her palms to his chest. "You can warm them on me. I'm burning up."

She nodded. "So am I. Inside, I feel as if a thousand fires are burning. Here." She touched his lips. "Here." She touched each of his nipples with a fingertip. "Here." She slid her hands down, past his waist, his abdomen. "Here."

Cade caught his breath as she touched him intimately. His body reacted eagerly, and he felt sixteen again with all of life still before him, his hopes high and certain.

"It's been a long time since I've felt like this," he told her, skimming the covers aside and gently pressing her onto the bed. Lying beside her, their bodies in full contact, he wondered if life had ever been this good or felt so right.

She touched his face so tenderly, he felt humbled by it and by the passion he felt for this woman, his childhood friend and long-lost sweetheart. When he smiled, she did, too. It did something to his heart, causing a strange ache inside that unpredictable organ.

Sara had never been so consumed by physical need, so driven to explore and excite another with every caress. A spark of wildness ignited her blood, and she writhed and moaned in his embrace, loving his masculine touch, the sensation of every part of her touching every part of him.

"Come to me," she demanded after hours, days, eons had passed in hot, desperate kisses.

He caught her wandering hands and held them captive against the mattress. "I will," he promised. "Give me a minute."

This time he was prepared, she saw, as he removed a packet from his jeans and affixed the condom in place. She held her arms up to him when he turned back to her.

"I didn't plan this far in advance," he murmured,

joining her again, "but I wasn't sure I could stop again if things got heated between us."

She nodded in understanding. "This time I don't want to stop."

He would have loved her for her honesty if nothing else. But there was more between them than the moment. A lifetime, he thought. A lifetime of waiting for her.

He moved over her, stroked her intimately, then slowly entered. Her quick inhalation told him how much pleasure she experienced as they merged into one.

"Yes," she whispered. "Cade, yes!"

Everything became centered on the two of them after that…sweet words, sweet kisses, then bliss… sweet, sweet bliss…

Feeling her climax, Cade let go the reins on his own passion and took his fill of her, thrusting again and again until he was spent, and even then he didn't want to stop, didn't want it to end. He felt her tense beneath him, then heard her little gasps of ecstasy as she responded to him yet again.

Pleasure, so deep and primitive it rocked his soul, shot through him. He wanted to shout in triumph as a sense of primal possession rolled over him.

After they regained their breath somewhat, he turned them to the side, still holding her close.

Sara laid an arm across him and rested her head on the pillow beside his. Outside the wind off the ocean blew around the cabin, but inside they were snug and safe.

"I don't think I've ever felt anything like that," he said, kissing along her temple.

He turned the lamp off and pulled the covers over their cooling bodies. She was glad. The dark hid the tears that slipped unbidden from her closed eyes.

"See how easy it is," Stacy shouted, looking back over her shoulder at the two adults who trailed behind her.

Sara nodded without loosening her grip on the reins or the saddle horn. Beside her, Cade chuckled.

"Try to relax," he encouraged. "You're hinged in the middle. Let the movement come from there."

"That's easy for you to say, but your muscles haven't frozen in position." She flashed him a quick smile as he laughed, then went back to concentrating on her horse's movements while she hoped the mare wouldn't make any sudden decision to run or something. "I may not be able to walk when I get off."

"The lighthouse isn't far," he said.

The Point Reyes lighthouse was their destination this morning. Stacy had knocked on her door at seven o'clock and told her they needed to get on their way in order to beat the crowd.

Sara had been startled out of a deep sleep and relieved to discover she was alone in bed. She'd slept so soundly she had no idea when Cade had left her side.

A funny, warm thrill ran over her as she thought of the night and the passion. The closeness afterward had been a surprise, an unexpected gift....

"Stop thinking like that." Cade's deep, quiet tone broke into her wayward musing.

He reached out and stroked her cheek as heat rose to her face. His smile was solemn even though a flame burned in his eyes.

She lifted her chin and told him, "I was wondering about the lighthouse and how lonely it must have been for the lightkeeper to live there day in and day out for years and years."

"Often a wife and family lived there, too."

During the ride, she questioned him about the ranch and how he'd come by it. He told her he'd used a legacy from his maternal grandparents as a down payment.

"Against my father's advice," he added ruefully. "He thought it was a waste of money, but Stace and I needed a place to stretch our legs."

"And to have the horses and dogs," Stacy had chimed in, circling back to them, then racing ahead again. She was a fearless rider and good at it.

Sara nudged the conversation to the jewelry business. By listening and asking a few questions, she learned the family wealth had come through his mother and her mother before that.

"Did you know my father and yours were in a partnership when we were little?" he asked.

A jolt of guilt hit her at the question. "I vaguely recall they were planning something."

"According to my father, they wanted to go after the really wealthy crowd—the crowned heads of Europe, billionaires and those types."

"That sounds rather ambitious. Did they have the assets for it?"

He frowned as he considered. "I suppose together they could have swung it. They were planning to make the most expensive necklace in the world out of matched, flawless diamonds. Unfortunately things didn't work out."

"My father drowned. I guess that ruined the plan."

She heard the bitter undertone, but couldn't take the words back. If her father had invested all his money in the diamonds and Walter Parks had kept them upon Jeremy's death, that would explain where her family's wealth had gone.

The mare tossed its head as if catching her agitation. Cade rubbed the animal's neck, which calmed it down.

"Aboard a yacht that belonged to my grandfather originally," Cade continued her thought. "I'm sorry for that, young Sara."

He spoke with such tenderness and compassion that the anger melted, leaving her feeling wounded and raw with guilt for wanting revenge.

Nodding, she urged the mare to a faster gait as Stacy waved impatiently for the two laggards to hurry. A few minutes later, they tied their mounts to a low branch on a scraggly cedar and walked to the crest of the hill.

From there the full vista of the sea spread before them like a painting. Seagulls wheeled overhead. Far away loomed the darker silhouettes of islands, barely visible on the horizon. A young couple walked down a long flight of steps toward the lighthouse on a promontory.

A park ranger stood beside a low building to her right. He smiled and spoke to them. A sign declared the area to be the Point Reyes National Seashore.

"Let's go down," Cade suggested. "Stace, hold the railing and don't run."

Sara held on, too. The stairs were steep and narrow. She noticed resting places at intervals along the side. "It's a long way down," she said over her shoulder to Cade.

"Three hundred steps. Just wait until we start back up." His smile felt as warm as the sun that caressed her shoulders as they descended.

They, along with the couple, explored the well-kept lighthouse from top to bottom. Stacy decided she wanted to live there when she grew up and turn the light on and off for the ships at sea.

By the time they returned to the crest—all three hundred steps—Sara was ready for a rest. They admired the colorful flowers of the lupine plants in the area and the orange mossy lichens on the rocks before mounting and riding back to the cottage along the cliff overlooking the beach.

They spotted the ranger setting up road signs in a parking area a mile from the lighthouse area.

"When the parking lot is full up here," Cade informed Sara, "he'll stop traffic down there until someone leaves, then the next in line can come up."

"I had no idea it would be that busy," she told him. "It seemed so isolated when we arrived."

"City dwellers like to get out on weekends. I don't blame them. If I didn't have the ranch to go to, I think I'd go stir crazy or something."

His eyes went dark for a second, then he smiled at her, which generated a ripple of electricity throughout her body.

For the rest of the day, they ate and played games and napped. In late afternoon, they helped the farmer and his two sons and two hired hands with the milking.

Stacy proved quite adept at washing the cows' teats in an iodine solution before the animals went into the milking parlor. Sara was conscious of four hooves near her head as she bent under the rounded bellies and followed the girl's instructions. The cows were on a platform three feet higher than where she stood, which conveniently brought the necessary parts close to hand.

Behind her, Cade chuckled each time she gave him a mock fearful glance as she did the chore.

"Good job," Stacy told her, obviously thinking her teacher needed some encouragement.

Cade suppressed a chortle as one sassy cow swung

her tail and slapped Sara upside the head, startling her and making her slosh the cup of antiseptic solution on the concrete.

"You'll pay for that," she assured him as she refilled the cup and dipped each fat teat in the liquid before wiping it down with a soapy cloth.

"This," he assured her, "will give you a deeper appreciation for farmers next time you're at the grocery."

When the cow whacked her again, Sara handed the washcloth to him. "You need to increase your own appreciation."

He stepped up and circled her with his arms, then expertly performed the task. "This is the queen cow," he said, looking over her shoulder, his mouth close to her ear. "She has two or three ladies-in-waiting who come in first to make sure it's okay. They always enter in the same order."

"What happens if another cow wants to be queen?"

"The ladies-in-waiting put her in her place."

Sara felt his chest move against her back as he chuckled, then he stole a quick kiss just under her ear before returning the cloth and moving back.

Her own breath caught, then she cleared her throat, gave him a warning glance, then waited as the gate to the milking room opened and the queen regally ambled through, her tail swinging from side to side. Another cow stepped forward, and Sara started the dipping and washing again.

"Thanks for the help," the farmer said when, after an hour, the three left the barn and returned to the cottage.

After grilling chicken strips and vegetable kabobs, they ate outside, the two dogs politely lying at their feet but keeping an eye out in case a morsel should happen to drop to the flagstone patio. Sara saw Stacy slip a couple of bites to each. So did Cade, but he pretended he didn't.

Sara smiled contentedly while her heart flitted around like a drunken butterfly as she waited for night to fall.

After Stacy's bath, Sara read her a story. The girl's bedroom was similar to the guest room in furnishings. A large teddy bear shared the bed with her. There was another bathroom upstairs and, of course, Cade's bedroom.

Sara had glimpsed a queen-size bed with an old-fashioned quilt over it in there. Tables with matching lamps were on either side of the bed. A cedar chest was next to the wall under a window. Scenes of a happy family preparing for the night after a busy day kept popping into her head.

"Ready for a back rub?" Cade asked Stacy, coming into the child's room when the story ended.

Sara moved to the end of the bed while he rubbed his daughter's back, then turned out the lamp and kissed her forehead. "Sleep tight."

"Don't let the bedbugs bite," Stacy replied. She yawned and pulled the cover to her neck. "Good night, Sara, I mean, Miss Carlton.'' She giggled, then closed her eyes.

Sara and Cade left the room, leaving the door ajar. He turned out the hall light when they reached the stairs.

At the bottom of the steps, he took her into his arms. ''Alone at last.''

His husky murmur was sexy and intimate. Sara wrapped her arms around his neck and met the kiss halfway. She, too, had been impatient for this moment.

His hands roamed her back, her sides, then moved between them to caress her breasts. She tilted her head back so he could reach all the sensitive places along her throat with his magic lips. When he slipped his hands beneath her and lifted, she swung her legs up and around his waist, clinging as he carried her to the privacy of the guest room and locked the door behind them before flicking on the lamp.

He sat in the cane-backed chair with her straddling his lap. With hands on her hips, he urged her to move against him. He was as ready for her as she was for him, she found.

When he smiled, she did, too, and felt a wrench deep inside, as if part of her already knew that the closeness of the day and the passion of the night were fleeting things, the elusive dreams of what might have been.

''You're thinking again,'' he scolded, touching the slight frown line between her eyebrows.

"I've never found it easy to live in the moment," she admitted. Or to deal with a guilty conscience, she added silently, wondering if he'd noticed her prying.

"Let's see what we can do about that," he suggested.

They kissed again and made love, then slept together until shortly before dawn. He woke her with his gentle touch and made love to her again. Later, she heard him in the shower, but she didn't get up until he called her and Stacy to join him for breakfast.

Then it was time to go back to the city.

"All good things come to an end," she murmured as they drove over the cow-guard and away from the ranch.

"I hope not," he said, smiling at her before facing the winding road back to the highway.

"We can come back next weekend," Stacy assured her.

Sara looked back before they turned onto the main road and she could no longer see the lovely rolling pastures of the ranch. Someone, she recalled, had written that a person couldn't go home again.

Once San Francisco had been her home, then her family had moved to Denver. With a child's acceptance of adult decisions, Colorado had become home. At the moment, she felt she didn't belong to either place.

What of the little paradise she'd shared with Cade and his daughter that weekend? Did she belong there?

She wanted to, she acknowledged, then sighed quietly as awareness stole over her. She'd foolishly done what she shouldn't. She'd fallen in love with the son of her enemy.

Chapter Seven

Cade went to the front door of his father's two-story Pacific Heights mansion while Stacy stopped to splash her hands in the Poseidon fountain in the front courtyard. He'd grown up in this house, but he felt no sense of nostalgia nor attachment to it.

His father had redone the interior some twelve or so years ago, removing the ornate furniture Cade remembered from his childhood and replacing it, with the help of an expensive decorator, with a minimalist style. The house now seemed like a store display—too sterile to house a family.

The door opened before he could ring the doorbell, and Brenda Wheeler, the housekeeper who'd raised Cade and his siblings, beamed at him.

"Wheelie," Cade said as he swept the matronly widow into an embrace and bussed her on each cheek.

"You rapscallion," she scolded, hugging him back. "Stop this foolishness and come in the house. Is that other rascal with you? I have a special treat for her in the kitchen."

"I'm here," Stacy called, running across the flagstones and up the steps. "What is the surprise?"

"Now that would spoil it, wouldn't it?" Mrs. Wheeler declared. "Mr. Cade, your father is waiting in the library. You come with me, missy."

Stacy went with the housekeeper while Cade directed his steps to the library, his favorite place in the fifteen-room mansion during his growing years. His father was there, a glass of wine in his hand, as he stood at the window and gazed at the night view of the city.

So was his sister, Emily. She stood at the bar, pouring a glass of wine for herself. "Cade, join us?" she asked, holding the decanter up.

He nodded. "Thanks, Em," he said, taking the glass, then leaning down to exchange a hug.

His twin had golden-brown hair, green eyes—which reminded him of another woman with brilliant green eyes—and their mother's dimples, which now deepened as she smiled warmly at him. Emily was a romantic. She denied it, but the facts belied her protests—she was a wedding planner. A very good one, according to their friends.

"I wondered if you would make it," Walter said,

crossing the room and stopping in front of Cade. "Your secretary said you'd left work early Friday and gone to the ranch."

Cade shook his father's hand and smiled in spite of the other man's sour expression and the fact Walter hadn't asked about Stacy, his only grandchild. "Of course I came. It's a command appearance, isn't it?"

He caught his sister's warning grimace, telling him their father was in no mood for jocularity. So? When had he ever been?

"Huh," Walter said and sat in his favorite chair. "I suppose we'll have to drag Jessica from her lair. Rowan hasn't yet informed me of his plans for the evening."

Jessica, the artist of the family, lived in a cottage on the estate. Her studio was there, and that's where she stayed unless otherwise summoned to the main house.

Rowan, the wild one, as Cade and Emily dubbed their brother, might or might not stop by. At that moment, Cade heard the roar of a motorcycle. "I believe he's here."

Emily smiled in relief. She, more than anyone, tried to keep peace between Walter and the children. Cade was glad she had her own place and a successful business. A hundred years ago, she would probably have lived at home, a spinster who had to bow to their father's orders.

Hearing voices in the back hall, Cade surmised Rowan and Jessica had arrived at the same time. He heard them both speak to the housekeeper, then her low voice urging them into the library.

Jessica came in first. She smelled of a floral perfume and the mineral spirits she used to clean her brushes. She was dressed in black from head to foot. The slacks and form-fitting knit top were striking with her blond hair and blue eyes. Like Em, Jessica also had Anna Parks's dimples and winning smile.

Rowan entered wearing jeans, boots and a ragged long-sleeved shirt over a black T-shirt. His hair was too long and he sported a three-day beard, all elements designed to irritate their sire. Like Jessica, he had blue eyes and dimples, but his hair was black as midnight.

Long ago, Cade had gotten used to Rowan's good looks stopping women cold in their tracks. Since the brothers had run in different circles, it hadn't been a problem.

"Cade," Jessica murmured, coming forward to hug him, then Emily. She spoke politely to the patriarch of the family, but that was all.

"Hey, bro," Rowan said in his irrepressible fashion. The two high-fived each other, then shook hands.

Of the four siblings, Cade thought his daughter took after Rowan the most in personality and high spirits, a fact that caused his brother to laugh uproariously in approval and conspire with the child to drive Cade up the wall on his rare visits to their house.

Rowan turned from Cade. His grin disappeared

when he looked at his father. "Father," he said in less than cordial tones and didn't offer to shake hands.

Walter nodded to his younger son.

Like emissaries from warring countries, Cade observed, each keeping a neutral stance while plotting the overthrow of the other.

"Wine?" Emily asked, breaking the little silence that hung over the room now that all were present.

"Got a beer?" Rowan asked.

"No, sorry." Emily gave him a beseeching glance, as if pleading with him to behave, then poured two glasses of wine and gave them to the younger pair.

When Mrs. Wheeler came to the doorway, Walter stood. "Dinner," he announced and held out an arm to each of his daughters.

Cade smiled grimly when Rowan waggled his eyebrows and fell into step beside him. They followed the other three into the dining room.

Assessing the others, Cade had a sudden sense of impending disaster. His father was unusually tense and dour, Rowan was obviously geared up for a fight, Jessica was oblivious, or indifferent, to all but her own dark thoughts, while Em probably hoped they could get through the evening with a modicum of grace and family unity.

Just another happy evening in his father's house.

As Jessica and Rowan became more and more silent, Cade and Emily kept the conversation going during the meal. He told of Stacy's new experiences in kindergarten and how much she liked her new teacher.

He explained about Tai and her mother's illness. "Sara has been taking Stace to school and keeping her every afternoon, so that's been a load off my mind."

"Sara Carlton," his father interrupted the story. "You took her to the ranch over the weekend."

At the accusing tone, all eyes turned toward Cade. "That's right," he said, forcing a calm he no longer felt. "I owed her for helping out."

"Big-time," Rowan agreed, giving their father a hard glance before finishing the last of his salad.

Mrs. Wheeler entered with the serving cart. She removed the salad plates, then served salmon and rice pilaf with a medley of vegetables and hot rolls.

"Is Stacy being a bother?" Cade asked.

"Not at all," the woman assured him. "She's had her dinner and is playing with the new kittens Tansy had. She's picked out the one she wants," she added with a smile before leaving the dining room.

"Stacy loves pets," Emily said to Cade. "Perhaps having a kitten will make up for having to leave the dogs and her pony at the ranch."

"What about leaving it at home alone all day?" he asked.

Jessica spoke up. "Cats are marvelously adaptable and easy to train." She glanced at Walter at the head of the table, bitterness in her eyes. "As are children."

Rowan held up his glass. "I'll drink to that." He finished off the wine.

To Cade's surprise, Walter merely glanced up, then continued eating, his mind evidently far from them.

When the meal was over, they returned to the library where Mrs. Wheeler had set up a tray with fresh coffee and a platter of various kinds of mints.

Cade, seated next to Emily on the sofa, wanted to collect Stacy and escape, but he sensed the evening wasn't over. The best or worst, according to how one looked at it, was yet to come.

"To what do we owe the pleasure of this little family get-together?" Rowan challenged as soon as the group was alone again. He poured another glass of wine, his fourth by Cade's calculation, and leaned an elbow on the mantel over the marble-tiled fireplace.

"Trouble," Walter said bluntly.

Emily and Jessica glanced at each other. There was no surprise on either face. They turned back to their father.

Walter perused one, then another of them, before he spoke. "There's a traitor among us."

"Father!" Emily said in shocked, scolding tones.

"It's true." Walter stirred cream into his coffee. He looked at Rowan. "Someone has been asking questions about the family, more specifically, our business dealings. And someone has been talking."

"What do you mean?" Cade asked.

"I mean there are questions being asked about our

personal affairs and…about things from the past. Old gossip is being stirred up.''

Cade noted the hesitation as his father picked his words, something that had been happening frequently of late when they discussed the state of the jewelry business.

What was Walter worried about?

The question startled Cade even as it leaped into his mind. He knew he'd hit upon some part of the truth—their father didn't want anyone delving into the past…because he was scared of what they might find out?

The icy hand of premonition glided down his spine. Something from the past was haunting the old man, but it wasn't ancient history that bothered Walter, Cade surmised. Instead, their father was worried about how this mysterious something from days gone by would affect the future. For some reason, Cade thought of Sara's father, who had once been Walter's partner.

''What kind of questions? What gossip?'' Rowan demanded.

''Ancient happenings that don't matter a damn,'' Walter said, dismissing the queries scornfully. ''I don't want anyone in this family telling any outsiders a thing. Is that understood?''

''No,'' Cade said before his brother could jump in, ''it isn't. Who are you worried about? What do you see as a problem from the past? What makes you suspicious that someone is probing into our business because of it?''

The familiar signs of anger suffused his father's neck and face in a dull red. An artery throbbed visibly near his temple. Cade maintained his cool.

Walter glared at him. ''Maybe the new neighbor that you're so taken with, for one. Her brother, for another.''

''Who the hell are you talking about?'' Rowan demanded.

''Jeremy Carlton's son and daughter,'' Cade answered, putting two and two together and not liking the way things were adding up. He felt defensive where Sara was concerned. ''Sara lives next door to me. Her brother is a detective with the SFPD. I don't know if you remember, but Carlton was Father's partner in an enterprise long ago.''

''He drowned,'' Emily said, her eyes widening. ''His body was never found. I remember how upset Mother was. There was speculation that he was murdered.''

''Mere rumors that don't bear repeating,'' Walter scoffed, his manner containing a warning and a threat. ''I've hired a private detective. If I find any of you have talked about the family or the business, I'll see that you're cut off without a penny.''

''God, I don't believe this.'' Rowan set his glass on the mantel so hard the stem cracked and a chip of crystal went flying across the expensive carpet. A pulse pounded in his temple, lending him the same

cold, calculating look of fury their father had sometimes turned on them over the years when they
pushed too hard or asked too many questions, especially about their mother.

"Afraid we'll let the world know our mother is in
a lunatic asylum in a foreign country?" the younger
son demanded, his voice just as scathing as the old
man's. "Afraid someone will find out your diamond
dealing isn't quite on the up-and-up as you would
have everyone believe?"

Walter surged to his feet. "Shut your mouth, boy,
or I'll shut it for you. I wouldn't be surprised if you
were stirring up trouble just for the hell of it."

The silence streamed like a force field throughout
the gracious room, binding the five of them in a mi-
asma of anger and resentment and dislike.

"Yeah," Rowan muttered. "Maybe that's exactly
what I've done. After all, I'm the black sheep of the
whole bunch, aren't I?" He glanced at his sisters, then
at Cade. "He's like a spider, wrapping everyone in
his web of control. I'd advise all of you to get out
while you still can. That's what I'm going to do."

"Rowan," Emily began worriedly.

"Don't say anything, Em," their younger brother
said bitterly. "Nothing would convince me to stay.
I'm outta here, like forever."

With that he left them, going down the hall and out
the back door without a backward glance. In less than
a minute, the roar of his motorcycle blasted the house
from the driveway, then faded into the night.

"Father," Jessica said. "I think you've gone too far this time." She rose and set her cup and saucer aside, but gently. "Rowan won't forgive you, and neither will I."

"It'll be a cold day in hell before I ask for forgiveness from my own children," Walter said coldly.

"Fine. I'm glad we had this little chat." Smiling rather defiantly she, too, left.

Cade stood. "You ready to go, Em?"

"Yes." Her lips trembled slightly as she tried to smile. "I'll say good night to Wheelie."

"Send Stacy out, will you?"

"Yes."

When they were alone, Cade turned to his father. "Is the house of Parks in trouble?" he asked, unable to hide the sardonic tone. "As your attorney, I need to know."

"No," Walter snapped. "Nothing's wrong. I'll explain things to Rowan next time I see him."

"I think," Cade murmured, heading for the door when he heard Stacy's voice in the hall, "that might be a long time. Stacy, come say good night to your grandfather."

When he and his daughter arrived home, Cade breathed a sigh of relief. He didn't know what the mess was, but he was damned sure his family was in deep.

After putting Stacy to bed, he went out on the back deck. The town house next door was completely dark.

Hell, he wasn't fit company tonight, anyway.

* * *

"I beg your pardon?" Sara said, staring at the principal of the Lakeside School for the Gifted on Monday morning. The woman's words made no sense.

"We are no longer in need of your services," her boss said again, her voice a monotone as if she read aloud from a dull script.

"Are you saying I'm fired?" Sara demanded in disbelief. "You can't fire me without cause. I have a contract."

The woman hesitated. "There's a clause in it relating to student enrollment."

"I have a full class."

"You'll receive payment for the semester, of course," the principal continued as if Sara hadn't spoken. "The secretary has the check. You may pick it up when you collect your things and sign out."

Sara started to protest further, but realized from the closed face across the desk that it was useless. Rising, she nodded with what dignity she could muster and went to clear her desk before classes started.

Fortunately she didn't have much this early in the school year. The supplies fit in one box that she could easily carry the three blocks to her town house.

When she went to the office to collect her check and sign out, Rachel was there, two bright red spots of anger in her cheeks. "I just heard," she said to Sara. "What is this all about?"

Sara shrugged. The school secretary pretended she couldn't hear a thing. She handed Sara an envelope and observed while she signed herself out. Under "reason for leaving campus," Sara put a question mark.

Rachel escorted her from the office to the front sidewalk. "This isn't right."

"No, but there's nothing we can do." Sara managed a smile. "You'd better go to your class. I don't want you in trouble because of me."

Her friend dismissed the thought with a wave. "I thought you and Cade were getting along rather well. Why would he have you fired?"

The question shocked Sara. "He wouldn't—"

She and Rachel stared at each other.

"Do you think Cade would have done this?" Sara asked after a moment of strained silence.

"Who else? He's on the board of directors. You know we always need good teachers. The old bat would sign away her soul before letting someone out of a contract, not to mention paying them a whole semester's salary for nothing."

Sara touched Rachel's shoulder, comforted that her friend was angry and indignant on her behalf. "Well, I suppose I'd better go before I get thrown off campus."

"I'll see you tonight. Let's go out to dinner," Rachel said. "Call your brother and see if he can come. We need to have a strategy meeting."

"Not tonight. Later this week. I'll call you," Sara promised, needing privacy to lick the wounds inflicted by this blow.

When Rachel nodded and retreated to her classroom, Sara started home. Glancing back as she approached the street corner, she saw a stranger standing at her classroom door, smiling and answering questions from the students when they realized Sara wasn't there.

She would have to return at three o'clock to pick up Stacy. Then…then sometime this evening she would tell Cade Parks exactly what she thought of him and his lying, conniving family. Like Rachel, she was convinced they were the ones who'd arranged this humiliation.

A frigid resolve entered her soul. She'd let herself get distracted by Cade and his charm, had fallen for his daughter and even thought she was falling for him, but she wouldn't be that foolish again.

Cade smiled at the warm leap of his heart when he pulled into the drive on his side of the duplex at nearly seven o'clock that evening. Home. And his two favorite girls waiting for him. He was eager to see them.

His day had been spent in a wrangle over a property settlement that had gone to civil court. Two brothers had started a business together. Now they'd had a falling-out. Such was the wisdom of doing business with family members.

As soon as the garage door was open, he pulled inside, parked and leaped up the steps leading to the kitchen.

"Hey, anybody home?" he called.

"We're here," Stacy responded. "We're drawing."

He tossed his suit coat and tie aside, then rolled up the sleeves of his shirt on the way to the deck. One glance at Sara chilled the warm glow inside him.

Although she was smiling, her eyes were as opaque as the cheap jade sold in tourist shops.

After going through the greeting ritual with his daughter, he turned to their neighbor. She held an artist's sketch book in her lap. On it was a pencil drawing of Stacy sitting on the deck railing, the city behind her and the Golden Gate Bridge beyond that.

"That's very good," he said, pausing beside her. "I didn't know you were an artist."

"I dabble," she said. "I'm not anywhere as good as your sister. I saw some of her work at a gallery today."

He tried to put all these pieces together and come up with a coherent picture. "Did you take your class on a field trip?"

She shook her head.

"We had a sub'tute," Stacy told him. "I didn't like her as much as Sara. None of us did."

"Substitute," he automatically corrected. "Sara is Miss Carlton to you," he reminded the child.

"She said I could call her by her first name since she isn't going to be my teacher anymore."

While his daughter gave Sara a disapproving glance for this latter sin, Cade added this information into the mix and still came up with a jumble. "This isn't making sense."

"I'm no longer employed at Lakeside," Sara informed him, her manner casual, her gaze cold.

The icy surety of knowing what was to come hit him like a flash flood in winter. "Why?"

She shrugged. "Apparently the class size wasn't big enough to sustain an extra teacher. That was the clause invoked to let me go. The good news is they gave me a check for my salary for the rest of this term. Nice, huh?"

"We'll talk about it later," he said, giving his neighbor a pointed perusal to assure her he meant to get to the bottom of this mystery.

Sara nodded, her head bent over the sketch as she went back to shading it with pencil strokes.

Stacy looked from one adult to the other. Cade knew his sharp-minded daughter had picked up on the undertones between him and Sara. It was time for a distraction.

"I'm starved," he said. "Let's go out for dinner."

"Sara and I already ate," Stacy told him, bridging the tense silence between the other two. "We had ice cream after school, and Sara got to meet Mrs. Ling. When Mrs. Ling held Mrs. Chong up next to Sara, their eyes were almost 'xactly the same. Raymond was there, too. He's in my class. Then we had Chinese."

Cade sorted through this information. Raymond was Mrs. Ling's grandson. Mrs. Chong was her cat, whose eyes indeed were as green as Sara's. The cat was also as aloof as Sara appeared at the moment.

"We got Chinese take-out," Sara clarified. "There's plenty left in the refrigerator for you." She stood. "I have some work to do. I'll see you in the morning, Stacy."

"Okay," Stacy said.

"Wait a minute." Cade tried to suppress his frustration while Sara gazed at him as if they were perfect strangers. Aware of his daughter taking every word in, he changed his mind about an interrogation at the moment. "I can drop Stace off on my way to work. There's no need for you to go to the trouble."

"As you wish."

With a nod to each of them, she sailed into her side of the mansion and closed the door.

"Do you think Sara is mad?" Stacy asked.

"I suspect she's tired. Come on, you can keep me company while I eat. Then it's bath time for you."

They went inside. By the time Stacy was in bed and sleeping like the angel children are purported to be, Cade was chomping at the bit to go next door and see what the hell was happening.

Sara thought of staying in her bedroom and not answering the door when she heard Cade's knock at the back of the house later that night. Reviewing her feelings as she went downstairs, she decided she was fine, all emotion bottled up and locked away.

"Come in," she said, standing back from the door after opening it at his impatient second knock.

She noticed he had the receiver for the monitor he kept in Stacy's room hooked to his belt. A thoughtful father, she scoffed. He looked after his own.

She sat in one of the chairs. He took the other.

The space between them, where the coffee table resided, was as wide as a canyon.

"What's happened?" he asked quietly.

"Nothing." At his ominous frown, she shrugged. "I was fired this morning. My services are no longer needed was the way it was put to me."

He regarded her with narrow-eyed scrutiny, then a light dawned in his eyes. "You think I had something to do with it."

She ignored the disbelief in his voice. "I'm positive of it." She wrapped her arms tightly across her middle as a shield from the tremors that had invaded her.

"Sara—"

"Was it your idea or your father's?" she asked, letting the glacier that had formed inside her penetrate her entire being, allowing icicles to coat each word.

Cade observed her without answering.

"It doesn't matter. I know where we stand now. I was distracted over the weekend," she admitted, the bitterness of the previous winter entering her soul. "But that won't happen again."

He rose. She did, too.

"What are you talking about?" he demanded.

"The mighty Parks family," she said scathingly. "You can have me fired, but nothing will stop Tyler and me from finding out the truth. We're not helpless children anymore, and we have friends in the city. You had better not try the same tactics on my brother."

The pleasant room filled with raging silence as they studied each other like opponents in a boxing ring. It would be a bare-knuckle battle to the finish, and only one of them would be standing at its end. That survivor would be her.

"What truth are you searching for?" he asked with a deadly calm that might have frightened her had she not been sure of her ground.

"The one involving my father, Jeremy Carlton, and your father, Walter Parks...the honorable Walter Parks," she mocked softly, "who was a liar, a thief, a seducer of other men's wives, a diamond smuggler..."

"Don't leave anything out," Cade invited when she paused, his voice as expressionless as his face.

She inhaled carefully, sensing his cold fury, then said, "Walter Parks, my father's partner. And his murderer."

Chapter Eight

Cade walked unannounced into Walter Parks's office at nine o'clock the following morning. The secretary followed uneasily behind him. "Mr. Parks is on a conference call," she repeated. "He isn't to be disturbed."

"It's all right, Connie," Walter said, placing the receiver on the hook. "I'm through with the call. Please close the door." It was an order, not a request.

She did so.

"Did I forget an appointment?" Walter asked.

Cade shook his head. "I have one question. Did you have Sara Carlton fired?" He knew the answer by the way his father's eyes darted away from him. "You did."

Walter shrugged. "I suggested to one of the directors that her services weren't needed."

"What else?" Cade demanded.

"Nothing."

The older man was lying. Cade knew it in his gut. The blood pounded through his temples at a furious pace. "What else?" he asked again.

"I suggested she might have an unsavory background, which she does," his father insisted at his snort of fury. "Her mother was an unstable person."

"Unstable," Cade repeated. "The way *my* mother was unstable and had to be sent away?"

"Not like that," Walter hedged. "Not exactly. Marla was given to depression and hysteria. She, uh, took things more seriously than warranted."

Cade digested the statement. "Such as the affair you had with her?" he asked softly, icy coldness joining the white-hot anger in his blood as he observed the familiar signs of anger in his father.

"I was not involved with her. Anyone who says so is a liar." A pulse pounded out of control in Walter's temple as his face suffused with color. "I suppose you've been listening to Marla's daughter."

Cade shoved his hands in his pockets and sat on the corner of the desk in a casual manner. "Yeah. We had an interesting conversation last night. She thought I'd gotten her dismissed and wanted to know if it had been my idea or yours."

Walter frowned. "What did you tell her?"

"Since I knew nothing of it, I didn't tell her anything."

"Good. Keep your mouth shut and this will all blow over in a day or two." He looked pleased.

"The way her father's death did twenty-five years ago?" Cade asked, keeping his tone neutral, his voice low.

There was a slight jerk to his father's hand before he waved it in dismissal. "That's ancient history. The police investigated thoroughly and concluded it was an accident."

"A convenient one," Cade murmured.

The flush spread from Walter's neck to his face. "What the hell are you suggesting?"

"You tell me."

The older man planted both hands on his desk and viewed Cade with narrow-eyed scrutiny. "Don't let the fact that you've got the hots for the girl get in the way of your thinking," he warned.

"So you had nothing to do with Jeremy Carlton's death?"

"No. It was like I told the police. We'd all had too much to drink while celebrating the new enterprise. I went to sleep. When I woke up, adrift on the tide, I barely got the yacht cranked up in time to avoid breaking up on some rocks. Jeremy was a fool to take the boat out on his own. We could have both drowned."

Cade considered the scenario painted by his father. It jibed with the police reports. But then, those reports used Walter's story to describe what happened. He shook his head slightly, not liking the way his thoughts were going or the faint shadow of doubt that nibbled at the edges of his mind.

"I can't believe my own son would ask me such a question," his father said, his voice rough with pain. "That was a horrible year, first with Jeremy's death and all the questions about it, then your mother's illness coming on top of that. With four children to raise, I was at my wit's end."

Cade felt a jab of guilt at bringing up old memories. "It was lucky we had Mrs. Wheeler by then," he said, recalling it had been the motherly widow who'd tucked them into bed at night and listened to their prayers.

"It was," Walter agreed. "With the business tangle to sort out after Jeremy's death, I had all I could do to keep the company solvent. Some of the diamonds we'd purchased were missing. We never found them."

"Sara and her brother think you kept the ones their father had bought."

Walter shrugged. "They would only see things from Marla's point of view. She even accused me of smuggling gems. Why would I do that when I had a perfectly legitimate business in diamond trading? The woman was crazy."

Cade mulled over the odds of there being two crazy women involved in the same scandal.

His father came around the desk and threw an arm

around his shoulders. "I don't know what Marla's kids think they hope to prove by stirring up the past, but I don't have anything to be ashamed of. I can assure you of that. You got time for lunch today?"

"Uh, not today," Cade said. "I'm swamped."

"Catch you another time, then," Walter said, jovial now that he considered their problem resolved.

Cade left the building and headed for his law office, aware of the cloud that sat over his head, its presence not quite letting him totally rely on his father's vow of innocence.

But why would he lie? What did he have to gain? More importantly, what did he have to lose?

Three hours later, Cade replaced the phone, noted the time used for the conference call on the charge sheet for that client, then stared out the window at the Golden Gate Bridge.

He had a corner office in the TransAmerica building in downtown San Francisco, so the view was impressive. As well as the bridge, he could see Alcatraz Island and the ferries plying the bay, carrying tourists to the prison so they could see where America's most notorious criminals were once housed. The Birdman of Alcatraz had been nothing like the movie version depicting him.

Neither, apparently, was Walter Parks.

An uneasiness rippled through Cade as he replayed that morning's visit with his father. A man was supposed to be considered innocent until proven guilty.

He certainly had no proof to the contrary on his father.

The conversation, argument, whatever, with Sara last night sloshed around in his brain like bile, bitter and burning in its intensity. The revelation of her true reason for moving to the city had haunted his sleep…which had been in moments, not hours, after he'd left her place and returned to his own town house.

His eyes felt like sand pits this morning, and his spirits weren't much better. Live and learn.

Sara wasn't the first woman who'd fooled him into thinking they had something special. His wife had done the same. He should have gained something from that first experience of betrayal.

He exhaled heavily, still not wanting to believe that the woman next door, the woman who had shared the sweetest moments in his arms, had done so only because she wanted information…and revenge on his father.

Sara had been sad at times. She'd seemed vulnerable and fragile, but there had been a core of honesty and openness about her. Stacy had trusted her at once, and he had trusted his daughter's instincts.

There had also been the connection between him and Sara as children—the shared kindergarten class, the disruption of their lives through no fault of their own by her father's mysterious death and his mother's equally mysterious departure. Those experiences had been life-altering for both of them and represented the same thing to the children they were at the time—abandonment by those they loved.

Over the weekend, they had shared more than childhood memories. Certainly she hadn't faked her response to their lovemaking. Or had she?

Hell, he couldn't tell truth from fiction anymore. He rubbed a hand over his face as if to shut out the pictures that rampaged through his mind. Sara smiling. Sara holding the saddle horn for dear life. Sara coming to him, meeting him eagerly as a lover—

"Hey, Cade, how about lunch?" a friendly male voice interrupted just as his thoughts were becoming uncomfortably steamy and his blood hot.

A distraction, that's what he needed to escape the morass his mind had fallen into. He nodded to Steve Knoles, fellow attorney and good friend at the law firm.

Like him, Steve had started with Clauson, Mason, Barnett and Raines, the senior partners of the company, right out of law school five years ago. Being the newest members of the prestigious group had bonded them from their first day. Their friendship had held fast from then on.

The two men walked to a nearby restaurant. Once they were seated and had gotten water and iced tea, Steve leaned close. "Can you keep a secret?" he asked.

Cade smiled wearily and crossed his heart. "To the grave."

Steve grinned, reminding Cade of Rowan when his

younger brother was in a devilish mood. Both men had blue eyes and dimples that melted the females of the species when they smiled. Steve wasn't quite as hotheaded, though.

"Something tells me this means trouble," Cade muttered to his friend.

"Nah." Steve waved aside the statement with feigned nonchalance. "I'm going out on my own. Want to be a partner in a new law firm?"

Cade blinked in surprise. "Run that by me again."

"I'm never going to make partner," Steve told him. "Old man Raines has hated me from day one. I've found a suite of offices in a good location. With the dot-com bust, rents are affordable, if I have a partner to share expenses. You, naturally, are my first choice."

"Hell's bells," Cade murmured. "Warn a guy before you hit him with something like this."

"Sorry. I've been thinking about it for a long time, but the cost was too high." He shot Cade a serious glance over the edge of his iced tea glass. "You'll make partner in a year or two, so it would be a greater risk for you to go out on your own than for me. That said, I hope you'll consider it seriously."

"Do I have time to think about it, or is this a do-or-die deal that has to be decided today?"

"Take all the time you need," Steve said airily, "but remember this—we would be our own bosses, determine our own hours, choose our own cases. Ah, the list is endless."

"Freedom," Cade said.

The word filled his head, luring him with a force stronger than any siren's call. In going out on his own, he would be free of his father's influence, his subtle threats and the demand for family loyalty.

Cade surveyed the proposal from every angle. His friend had certainly provided the distraction he'd needed from his own gloomy thoughts. Freedom. The temptation of it.

He admitted it had daunted his ego when the old man had made it clear Cade's position came through the Parks name rather than his own record of achievement.

Which was excellent, he grimly reminded himself. He'd been an honor student and had graduated third in his class. At the law office, he'd done well and earned a reputation as an able attorney. Bringing the Parks account to the firm had been a plus for him, but he'd never considered it worth more than his own merit—

"Earth to Cade," his friend intoned. "Are you envisioning us on our own, arguing cases like Perry Mason and supplying the damning evidence at the last moment?"

"Right," he said dryly. "Who's going to be Paul and Della to our combined Perry?"

"I know a private detective," Steve said. "He did some work for a client of mine last year. Mark Banning. You ever hear of him?"

Cade shook his head. "Don't think so."

"If he came in with us, we could move to a bigger place. I'm thinking of specializing in insurance and medical fraud. A detective in-house would be just the thing."

Cade studied the other attorney. "Why do I get the impression you've thought this through, and all the detective and I need to do is sign the lease papers?"

Steve flashed a supremely satisfied smile. "You're really going to consider it?" he asked. At Cade's nod, he muttered, "Hot damn!"

"I'm not signing on the dotted line yet, but yes, it's something to think about. In fact, I may have use for your friend's services."

The waiter stopped by to take their order. After he left, Steve gave Cade a quizzical glance.

"I want information on something that happened a long time ago. Twenty-five years, in fact." He leveled a serious stare at his friend. "Can you keep a secret?" he asked.

Steve nodded. "To the grave," he vowed, repeating Cade's earlier promise.

"Things seem to be getting serious," Tyler muttered to Sara while dipping sushi in hot wasabi sauce.

She nodded in agreement. He'd called last night and asked her to meet him for lunch today after she'd told him about her dismissal and her accusation toward Cade and/or his father for it.

"Have you decided when you're going to confront Walter Parks about yours and Conrad's paternity?"

"Not yet. I want to find out more on his dealings with Jeremy. Ah, there's Robert."

Sara followed her brother's line of sight and saw a man in a conservative suit speak to the hostess, then head their way. "Who is he?" she asked.

"Robert Jackson, from the D.A.'s office. He prosecuted the murder case I investigated back during the spring. I thought we should ask his advice and invited him to lunch if he had time."

Before she could voice any opinion about this, the man arrived at their table. Tyler made the introductions and invited the attorney to be seated.

"Glad you could join us," Tyler said. "Anything new on the Shrimpton case?"

The assistant D.A. shook his head. "The trial has been delayed for the third time while the defense is searching for a witness. They've hired Mark Banning to help. I think you know him, don't you?"

"Sure, he's my partner's brother."

While the men talked, Sara estimated the newcomer's age to be in the mid-to-late thirties. He had a permanent crease across his forehead and a few strands of gray in his black hair. His manner was intensely serious. She found that reassuring, as if he meant business and would let nothing stand in his way while getting at the truth of a situation.

"What's happening with you?" Robert asked after snagging the waiter and placing his order.

"We need your advice," Tyler admitted, lowering

his voice. "It's about a paternity case, for one thing, and about murder, for another."

"An interesting combination," the assistant D.A. murmured. "Murder I can help you with. Paternity is a civil suit ordinarily. Unless it's directly involved in the murder."

While the trio ate, Sara and Tyler put forth all the information they had gleaned from their mother and added in the details of their research since moving to San Francisco.

"Mark and Nick Banning are helping us find this long-lost uncle," Sara told the assistant D.A.

"Derek Ross, or Moss or whatever he calls himself, witnessed the crime," Tyler finished the tale.

"You have to locate him, or else there's no case," Robert said, echoing their conclusions. "You need some kind of evidence to show a motive. Usually greed is a good one. What would Walter have gained by eliminating Jeremy?"

"The rare diamonds Jeremy had already invested most of his assets in?" Tyler suggested. "They were never recovered that we know of."

"You have any kind of proof that these diamonds actually existed and that your father bought them?"

"No. We think Walter kept them and used them to start his jewelry stores," Sara told the attorney. "That was why Jeremy's business was in serious debt and went under when he died. Everything had to be sold to pay for merchandise that apparently never existed or was never found, at any rate."

"A bum deal," Robert said sympathetically.

"That's what we think, too," Tyler said, his expression grim and much older than his years.

Sara forced back the anger that threatened to erupt as she gazed at her brother. It had been a long time since she'd seen him carefree and happy as a young man his age should be. He should be thinking of falling in love and getting married and having a family, but because of Walter Parks, that life had been denied all of them.

She and Tyler had established themselves in San Francisco while riding high on a wave of righteous indignation, but life was so much more complex than one emotion, she'd discovered. She suspected her brother had found out the same thing.

While he'd had a rather serious relationship with one woman, they had broken up because of his vow never to marry and have children. Their mother's unhappiness had touched all the Carlton children in various ways, none of them leading to a trusting relationship with another human.

She sighed quietly and gazed out the window while Tyler and the attorney discussed how to handle a paternity suit and whether to go ahead with it before finishing the murder investigation. Suddenly, down the street, she recognized a tall, lithe masculine form.

Cade and his companion were deep in serious discussion as they hurried along the sun-filled avenue.

Her heart lurched so hard, she put a hand to her chest to hold back the pain. Not for the first time, she was sorry she'd ever moved to this city. And sorry that she'd met Cade Parks and discovered the man of her dreams.

Yes. She regretted that most of all.

Later that afternoon, Sara sat at a computer in the local library. Noting the date that came up on the screen, she realized that tomorrow she would have been in San Francisco for three weeks.

Three weeks. So short, yet she felt she'd compressed a lifetime into those twenty-one days.

Forcing her attention to the job at hand, she typed in the names she wanted to review. The computer searched the archives of the local newspaper and came up with a surprisingly large list of selections.

She read of Walter Parks's marriage to Anna Lindsay, daughter of a gem-mining, trade and exploration tycoon. Walter had been thirty, the bride, beautiful and glowing with happiness, only twenty.

Staring at the picture of Walter in his wedding tux, Sara's heart tightened into a painful ball. Cade looked very much like his father.

That didn't mean he was like his father in personality, some part of her argued.

She shut out the quarreling halves of her heart and concentrated on the articles. Arthur Lindsay had died two years after the marriage. By then the twins, Cade and Emily, had been born. Next had come Rowan, then Jessica, in quick succession. After the final birth announcement and a few charity functions, Anna

Lindsay Parks apparently disappeared from the face of the earth.

Sara closed her eyes and replayed her mother's dying accusations and agitated murmuring. Yes, Anna had been at the celebration party Walter had thrown aboard his yacht. Walter, Anna, Marla and Jeremy were present, along with Marla's younger brother, Derek Ross, and a few other staff people involved in the diamond-trading business with Walter and Jeremy. Before the joint enterprise, Carlton's company had been the biggest rival of Parks Mining and Exploration.

That was one way to get rid of the competition, Sara mused. Join forces, then make sure the other man faded from the scene. The ink had hardly dried on the contract of the joint endeavor when Jeremy conveniently drowned, leaving Walter in charge of everything.

The newspaper article stated that after the celebration party was over, Walter and Jeremy had stayed on board to drink a final toast to the success of their joint effort. Someone from a neighboring berth in the marina saw the yacht leave its moorings and head out for another cruise.

Later, in a statement to the police, Walter reported that he'd had too much to drink and had fallen asleep. When he awoke, the boat was drifting aimlessly at sea near the dangerous currents by the Golden Gate Bridge. Perplexed, he brought the yacht back into the harbor.

When he later discovered his new partner was missing, Walter could only surmise that Jeremy, equally intoxicated over their potential success, had taken the boat out, then fell overboard at some point during the night. There had been no one to dispute Walter's word, so the tragedy had been marked up as an unfortunate accident.

Sara shook her head in anger and frustration. Derek had also been aboard the yacht when it went out the second time, according to her mother's story. He'd gone to sleep in a cabin and was awakened by the quarrel between the two men. He heard Walter admit he was smuggling diamonds into the country. Opening the door to the main salon a crack, he saw Jeremy apparently pass out, then Walter had started up the yacht and headed out to sea.

Not sure what was going on, Derek had stayed in the dark cabin. When the engine slowed to an idle, he had witnessed Walter drag Jeremy onto the deck, then had heard a splash. Walter had returned to the salon, washed the used highball glasses, then returned to the wheel.

After they'd arrived at the marina and Derek was sure Walter had left, he sneaked out and went home. Later he told Marla what he'd seen. Marla had told him to keep his mouth shut if he didn't want the same thing to happen to him.

Sara rested her forehead on her clasped hands as the bitterness surged and burned in her. Greed begat violence. Maybe her family had been better off without wealth.

"Are you all right?" a soft voice asked.

Raising her head, Sara stared at the young woman seated at the next computer. She managed a smile and nodded. "Just thinking," she said.

"Well, that can be difficult," the other woman admitted in a rueful tone.

Sara laughed with her, then quickly read all the other articles on Walter Parks and his family up to the present day. There wasn't much information. The family had maintained a low profile with the press, it seemed, since that fatal incident. The yacht, according to Mark Banning, had been sold once the investigation had closed.

Interesting.

Sara closed the files and signed off. Any doubts that had lingered over her mother's story were now laid to rest. Walter's story didn't hold water, one might say.

An hour later, Sara met Tai on the front walk to the school. "Hi," the medical student said, looking embarrassed. "Uh, I came by to pick up Stace. My mom is doing fine, so I'm back on the job."

"That's good news," Sara said warmly. "I'm no longer teaching here, but I've been picking up Stacy in the afternoons."

"Yeah, Cade called and explained…sort of." The student gave Sara a questioning glance.

The bell rang. Sara backed up a step. "I'll leave

you to it, then," she said and hurried along the street, heading home before the youngster spied her and insisted she join her and Tai. Sara didn't feel up to cheerful chatter.

At the house, she stayed inside with the doors closed, like a criminal hiding out after a robbery. It wasn't until well after dark that she ventured onto the back deck, needing fresh air and freedom from her own company and the thoughts that went round and round in her head.

She stiffened when the door opened behind her. The lights had been off next door, so she'd assumed Cade was in bed. It was almost eleven o'clock. Huddling deeper in the afghan she draped over her shoulders, she hoped he wouldn't notice her.

"Hello, Sara," he said quietly. "Are you in hiding?"

"Yes."

His chuckle wasn't one of amusement. There was anger in it, and a cool detachment she hadn't heard before.

He sat in one of the deck chairs. She sensed him gazing her way. Reluctantly she turned her face to him.

"Where do we go from here?" he asked.

"I don't know. Nowhere, I guess."

"No," he said, disagreeing. "Things have gone too far for that. I talked to Mark Banning this afternoon."

"Mark," she repeated, trying to decide what this meant.

"I want him to check on certain things for me. It seems he's already been doing that."

Sara was pretty sure she knew what was coming, but she kept her mouth shut.

"He knew a lot about my family," Cade concluded, still in that same quiet, coolly controlled tone.

His very air of calm made her nervous. He should have been openly furious or something. Instead he seemed remote and above it all. However, she'd grown up with her mother's unpredictable moods, so she wasn't sure.

"His brother works with mine," she finally murmured after the silence lasted too long.

"So he said."

"Then...you know everything."

"I think so," he admitted. "Like you, I think it's time we laid these old ghosts to rest."

She wasn't taking anything for granted. "What do you mean?"

"I want to help you and Tyler with your investigation."

She shook her head. In the dim glow of the city lights, she saw him nod affirmatively. "We don't need help."

"I think you do. Who would be better at researching family history than the family attorney?"

Clutching the afghan in shaking hands, she shook her head again. "Walter Parks is your father."

The pause was brief. "I know."

"I never wanted to hurt you." She realized how

lame that sounded. "I didn't think about it like that," she said, "in terms of pain and loss to others. Tyler and I wanted justice for our family. That was all."

"Justice," he echoed, a wealth of irony in the word. "I'll help you find it. This shadow has been hanging over our lives for twenty-five years. I agree with you and your brother. It's time we dispelled it."

Questions raced through her mind, but she didn't ask any of them. They sat there in tense silence. Traffic noises came to them at intervals as an occasional vehicle drove down the neighborhood street.

"Mark didn't tell me much," Cade continued. "He said it wasn't his story to tell. Will you fill me in? I need to know what evidence you have or what you're trying to find out, in order to help."

"I can't tell you, not without speaking to Tyler first. It's his story even more than mine." She couldn't tell him why—that her half brother was also his half brother.

The tension became unbearable before Cade nodded. "I understand."

"I don't think so." Her heart hurt, physically hurt, as she thought of him and his siblings and her own. He wouldn't believe the duplicity of their parents—his father's crime and her mother's silence.

"Do you have a witness?"

She was so startled by the question, she could only stare at him. That action was enough to give her away.

"There was," he concluded. "Or you think there was. Who was it?"

Sara's heart pounded like a runaway train. She pressed her lips tightly together as if the answer might escape before she could stop it. She had her own questions about the past and its strange connections.

Why hadn't Marla brought her brother forward all those years ago and had Walter convicted for his crime?

Even though Marla had expressed her fears of the man, obviously for good reason, her silence was something Sara would never understand. Of course, there had been the pregnancy and the twins that belonged to the murderer. That added to the tangle.

"You're afraid to tell me. Do you think I'll tell my father and that he'll murder him, too?" Cade asked with more than a tinge of sardonic amusement in his voice.

"No," she denied, but her voice quivered, betraying her doubts. "It's so complicated, so unbelievably complicated," she murmured, drawing her knees up and wrapping her arms and the afghan over her legs as if to hold the tide of misery at bay. She sighed despondently.

He observed her huddled form before speaking. "We'll sort one thread out at a time."

"And then?"

"And then we'll see."

"I hate it when children are involved," she told him.

He hesitated. "I heard Stacy tell you she didn't like visiting her grandfather. She said he didn't like people."

"I didn't encourage her to talk about him," Sara quickly said.

Cade waved aside her remark. "I don't think she'll be surprised or particularly upset by anything that happens to him. He hasn't earned her affection."

That struck Sara as the saddest thing of all. Children should have loving grandparents that thought they hung the moon. Her own had died before she was born or before she'd been old enough to remember them. She'd always felt she and Kathleen and the twins had been cheated out of something important because of that.

"I think you should stay out of it," she said to Cade.

"I can't. We're too deeply involved."

She lifted her head and stared at him. He returned it, his face grim and determined.

"Will you set up a meeting with your brother?" he asked. "And Mark Banning and his brother. Is there anyone else in on this?"

"Rachel knows some of it," Sara admitted. "She helped me get the town house..." Realizing she might have said too much, Sara let the words trail off.

"Yes, I'd already figured a bit of collusion there."

"I didn't plan the rest," she said in a low voice. "What happened between us, the visit to the ranch and...and everything."

He stood and paced the deck like a caged beast. "That's good to know. For a while, I thought maybe you'd faked your response, then I decided you hadn't. It was too compelling for either of us to pretend."

"I didn't expect it. The passion, the terrible need, like lightning inside me." With an effort, she stopped the futile confession. "It was unwise."

"But good," he murmured, so quietly she could hardly hear. "So very, very good."

They observed each other without speaking for a full minute. Torrents of hunger surged between them like a storm tide caused by an angry god, bent on vengeance.

Sara stood it as long as she could, then she fled inside and locked the door behind her, not to keep him out but to remind herself that she must stay in. His arms were not the safe haven she sought.

There was no safe place, she realized, until the past could be exposed, then decently buried for all time.

Chapter Nine

"I didn't tell him anything," Sara assured Tyler when he returned her call, an hour after she'd fled from Cade and her conscience and left a message on his phone. "Except that we think Walter killed Jeremy. And that we want to see justice done. He volunteered to help us get the truth."

"Huh," Tyler said in a skeptical voice.

"He wanted to know what evidence we had. He, uh, seemed to think we had a witness."

That brought a more forceful response. "The hell he did! What did you say? You didn't tell him about our search for Mom's brother, did you?"

"No, I didn't mention the lost uncle. I told him it was more your story to tell than mine. He wants a meeting with everyone who's working on the case. You, Nick, Mark—oh, Cade apparently spoke to Mark earlier today.''

''What for?'' Tyler demanded. ''I don't like the sounds of this. Too many people are getting involved. We may as well hire a sandwich-board guy to walk around town and advertise what we're doing.''

''I think he wanted Mark to investigate something.'' She paused to consider. ''Us, most likely.''

''Great,'' Tyler muttered in disgust. ''I'll call Mark… No, it's after eleven. I'll call him and Nick first thing in the morning. Can you set up a meeting at your place for tomorrow night? Nick and I can get there by eight.''

''Make it nine,'' she told him. ''Cade is busy getting his daughter to bed before then.''

''Okay, nine it is.''

''Should I include Rachel?''

There was a brief silence. ''Why?''

''Well, she basically knows everything and wants to help. I don't know if she can contribute anything, but she and Nick worked together to get me into the duplex.''

''Hell, the more, the merrier,'' her brother said. ''I'll call the mayor and see if he can join us, too.''

''Maybe we ought to ask Walter Parks.''

''Sure. Why not? We can just ask him point-blank if he did the dastardly deed.''

Sara smiled at Tyler's snort of sarcastic laughter. Their quest had taken on the air of old-fashioned melodrama. On this note, they said good-night and hung up. She called Rachel. Her friend was still up. Sara brought the other woman up-to-date.

"Darn, I have parent consultations tomorrow night," Rachel complained. "It'll be well after nine before I wrap that up, so I won't be able to make it. Keep me informed, will you?"

Sara promised she would.

After turning off the bedside lamp, she stared at the dark ceiling until her eyes felt like sandpaper. Last winter, time had ticked by slowly while she'd waited at her mother's bedside for the inevitable end. Now it seemed to be rushing forward way too fast, the hours whipping by until she wanted to ask for a reprieve and have the moment stand still while she sorted things out—how she felt, how she thought she should feel, what she wanted to happen.

One thing for sure—she wanted all of this scheming and searching to be over. She wanted a future without questions or doubts plaguing every decision she made. She did not want to live in "interesting" times.

Serenity. Was there such a thing?

Cade stood at the rear door of his town house. It was twenty minutes before he was due next door. Stacy had fallen asleep before the end of the story, so he had the time to himself, as unusual as that was. Every minute of every day seemed to be taken up with obligations.

Restless, he went out on the deck and sat on the railing. The breeze off the ocean brought the tang of salt to him. He thought of sailing off into the unknown and not coming back. A life without complications was tempting.

Hearing movement in the other town house, he turned so he could see inside. Sara came into the den and placed a tray loaded with egg rolls, pot stickers and lots of veggies on the coffee table, then returned to the kitchen without glancing outside.

She was dressed in black slacks with a pink silk shirt. A black-and-pink scarf held her hair from her face. He observed the movement of her slender form until she disappeared from sight. Unbidden memories flooded his mind.

He'd explored and caressed every inch of her lissome body during their weekend at the ranch. She'd done the same to him. They'd discovered each passionate nook and cranny of the other in those stolen hours. They'd shared the quiet, contented afterglow of making love.

Had it all been a lie? Or was she as frustrated by their conflicting relationship as he was?

Heat spiraled low in his body. Whatever else lay between them, that part hadn't changed. He wanted her with a hunger that surprised and annoyed him. With every thought of her, the familiar longing blazed through him like lightning striking a dry forest. Passion had been the downfall of many men, he reflected. Going to the door, he knocked softly.

''Come in. The door's unlocked,'' she called, returning to the den with another tray stocked with fruit, several kinds of cheese and an assortment of crackers.

She wore a worried expression, and tension was evident in the line of her shoulders. He could identify with that.

''Is this a meeting or a party?'' he asked with a certain rueful edginess to the tone.

''Tyler is always hungry,'' she explained.

She glanced at him, then checked the trays, her manner so serious, he felt a quixotic urge to take on her burdens and ease the load she carried. He silently laughed at the ridiculous notion. He wouldn't be a fool for a woman again.

''Looks good, young Sara,'' he said, forcing a smile.

Pausing, she studied him as if puzzled. ''Why do you call me that?''

He shrugged. ''I think the young girl I once knew is still there, hidden behind the turmoil and grief and injustice of a grown-up world.''

She shook her head. ''She's gone, Cade. She disappeared a long time ago.''

''Perhaps.'' He knew he should leave well enough alone, but something prodded him to add, ''She lives in my heart if nowhere else.''

The golden flecks in her green eyes flashed in the lamplight. She blinked tears back with visible effort.

''She lives in a boy's dreams,'' she corrected, giving him a defiant glance. ''Not in the real world.''

"Last weekend seemed pretty real to me."

A blush crept up her neck. "That was wrong—"

He wasn't going to let her brush the weekend aside that easily. "No, it was the one thing that was right. Everything else may be wrong, but that wasn't."

"If only life were that simple."

"Yeah. If only," he agreed, forcing himself to ignore the forlorn sadness in her eyes. He shrugged. "Maybe it can be, once we resolve the past and its problems."

"If we can," she said.

The three simple words expressed all the doubts she didn't voice. He wanted to argue with her, but what was the point? She was right.

The ring of the doorbell stopped the conversation. Sara rushed from the room to answer it. Cade heard more than one male voice. Her brother and his friends had arrived.

He moved so that he could see down the hallway. Sara turned from hugging her brother and hugged the other two. He felt a strong stab of jealousy at her ease with the Banning brothers and reprimanded himself for it.

Perhaps in another life in another time, he and Sara would have met and loved in the natural order of things, but not in this lifetime. Too much stood between them.

The gods must be laughing.

"Cade," Sara said, leading the way to the den, "you've met Tyler and Nick. This is Mark Banning.

You said you'd spoken to him earlier. Have you two met?''

"Only by phone," Cade said, stepping forward to shake hands with each of the men. The older Banning had a pretty serious scar under his right eye. Cade wondered if that was why he'd left police work and opened his own agency.

"Please make yourselves comfortable," Sara invited. "Tyler, there's an assortment of drinks on the island. Do you mind playing host?"

"Not at all, sis." The brother followed her to the island and called out choices to the men, then prepared wine, beer, iced tea or coffee, as they preferred.

Watching brother and sister work together, Cade was reminded of his idealistic version of marriage before his eye-opening experience with wedded bliss and the reality he'd discovered after the ceremony.

His wife had expected maids and caterers to do all the work. She'd been furious that he'd expected them to live on what he made. A law student's earnings, then a newly fledged attorney's salary didn't match her aspirations at all. Neither did his idea of living in an apartment while they saved to buy their own place.

Interestingly, she and his dad had gotten along quite well. She'd wanted to live in the ornate mansion in Pacific Heights. Cade had refused.

Being around Sara brought back old dreams of having a warm, loving family. At four, that's what he'd thought his own family had been. It was only after his mother was gone that he'd realized it had been

Anna who'd made the children feel loved and wanted, not his father.

Glancing at the four pairs of eyes on him, he realized Sara and the men expected him to start this meeting, or whatever one called it.

"I suppose we should begin with what we know," he said. "Sara and Tyler are trying to solve a twenty-five-year-old mystery regarding their father's death." He paused as Sara and Tyler glanced at each other. Neither spoke, so he continued, "Since the event, whether an accident or something more sinister took place on my father's boat, that quest involves my family. I, too, want to know the truth about the drowning."

"Why?" Tyler challenged.

Cade met the brother's hard gaze, then glanced at Sara. "Because it hangs over our heads like a cloud that never goes away. I think the questions from the past must be cleared up so we can all go forward with our lives."

Tyler looked skeptical. "Even if we prove your father was the perp?"

Cade nodded. He'd read the newspaper reports and had reconciled himself to the worst possible scenario. "I assume you have some kind of evidence, or else you wouldn't have uprooted and moved here."

"We're working on it," Tyler affirmed.

"With the help of your friends." Cade gestured to the Banning brothers.

"Maybe," Tyler said.

"I can help."

The brother looked skeptical. "How?"

"I probably know more about my father's business than anyone else."

"You know about Parks Fine Jewelry. Your father has another attorney for his personal business."

Cade returned Tyler's challenging stare. "As he should, since I am an heir to his fortune."

"His ill-gotten fortune," Sara said, anger darting through her expressive eyes.

"So that's what it comes down to," Cade murmured. "Money, always money."

"That's usually the problem," Mark Banning agreed. "But in this case, a man lost his life. We want to understand how and why."

"So do I," Cade said coolly. "It looks as if we're all on the same wavelength here."

"Yeah? We don't intend to deal you in just yet," Tyler told him.

Cade wasn't surprised at the younger man's suspicions. His being involved was rather like inviting the fox to guard the chicken house. "It would speed things along if I knew what we were looking for."

"When we find some solid evidence, we'll let you know," Tyler said.

"In the arrest warrant, I presume?" Cade hadn't really expected the group to confide all to him, but he had hoped for some cooperation. "My father has gotten wind of questions being asked about him and his business. He knows you two are in town." Cade gave Sara and Tyler a pointed glance. "I think he's prepared for trouble."

His eyes were drawn to Sara, sitting so silent and looking so remote. Whatever happened, there wasn't a future for them. So what else was new?

Sara listened to the men's conversation and observed the interactions between them. Her brother wasn't about to confide in Cade. Tyler stopped just short of being openly hostile about the other man's motives.

Nick and Mark Banning were noncommittal. Mark shared the information he'd found on the case. It was gleaned from the same newspaper reports that she'd read in the library and contained nothing new. The detective didn't mention the missing uncle to Cade, she noted.

At ten o'clock, Cade left, going out the back door as usual.

Tyler studied her as he filled his plate with second helpings of everything. "Do you trust him?"

She thought it over before answering. "In the dealings I've had with him since moving here, and in watching him with Stacy, he seems to be honest and sincere."

"But it's his father we're talking about putting behind bars," Mark said, voicing everyone's concern.

"I don't think they're close." She pressed her fingertips to her temples, where a dull headache had formed. "I can't say I was close to my father, either.

He worked long hours, so we rarely saw him, other than brief periods on the weekend. But I loved him.''

She looked at Tyler. Her brother had never known a father's love and never would. No matter what DNA tests showed, Walter Parks wouldn't want his unknown sons.

''Don't feel sorry for me,'' Tyler told her, correctly reading her thoughts. ''With Walter Parks for a father, I haven't missed anything. I don't think Cade has, either.''

''What do you mean?'' she asked.

''I suspect Walter is only interested in his children as a means to his own ends. From what I've learned about the man, no one gets in his way, not even his own flesh and blood.''

''He must be a horrible person,'' Sara murmured, thinking of Cade and his relationship to the elder Parks. ''I want to see him locked up so he can't hurt anyone else.''

''Well, until we find your uncle, we don't have anything to go on,'' Mark reminded them. ''I've widened the search for him, but with all the separate towns, each with its own records, surrounding the San Francisco area, it's going to take time to get through all the deeds and tax records.''

''I can help,'' Sara volunteered. ''I need something to fill my time since I'm no longer gainfully employed.''

''Tyler and I can adjust our work schedules and pitch in, too,'' Nick spoke up. ''With four of us searching for Derek Ross, we'll find him if he's any-where in the city or the outlying areas.''

"Right," Tyler said grimly. "It's only a matter of time."

Sara joined the men in plotting the search. Each of them agreed to inspect the records of the various sub-urbs around the city, looking first at the owners of bookstores for clues to the missing relative.

"I wonder what he's like," Sara said when the men were leaving. "He was twenty-two when it happened, according to Mother. That would make him around forty-seven now. I wonder if he ever married and had a family." She looked at Tyler. "His children would be our first cousins. We may never meet them."

"We will," Tyler vowed, looking stubborn. "We'll find Derek. This time he won't slip away be-fore we can question him. We'll make him tell us the truth."

The Thursday-afternoon traffic was heavy when Cade and Stacy started for home after taking care of their shopping. He took the coast road, a much more pleasant drive than going directly through the city.

Even here, the street was more congested than usual. However, maintaining an even thirty-five miles an hour, he got through the traffic lights without hav-ing to stop after passing the Cliff House.

At the duplex, he parked in the driveway and noted that Sara's car was in the other one. A tightness invaded his chest, while hunger and a yearning he couldn't name clamored inside him. He hadn't expected a lot from the meeting with her brother and friends last night, and he hadn't gotten a lot. Given the circumstances, he could hardly blame them.

For himself, while he knew his father was ambitious and competitive, those traits were far from the calculated ruthlessness it would take to murder someone.

On the other hand, the circumstances surrounding Jeremy Carlton's death were too strange to be ignored. He, too, felt a need to delve into the past and sort truth from fiction and supposition.

If they did prove Walter had murmured his partner, then what? Cade saw only a black hole where the future should be.

"Sara's home," Stacy announced. "I've got to show her my kitten. She can help me name her."

Cade started to tell his daughter to leave their neighbor alone, but thought better of it. Stacy considered Sara her friend. There was no sense in expecting a child to understand adult complications. He would let the girls work it out between them.

Stacy carried the basket that contained the eight-week-old black-and-white kitten while he opened doors for her. She rushed through the town house to the deck.

"Sara, look what I have," Stacy called as she exited and left the door open behind her. "A kitten. What shall we name her?"

"Let me see her, then maybe we can think of

something really good," Sara said. "Oh, how pretty. Look at those blue eyes, Stace. What's something that goes with them?"

Cade left the kitten's food in the kitchen and set up a litter box in the guest powder room. Wheelie had assured him the kitten knew how to use it. He and Stacy had bought kitty supplies, including the basket to sleep in, and toys at a pet store after the house-keeper had called and said the kitten was ready to come home with them.

"I don't know," he heard his daughter say. "What's something blue?"

"Violets are blue-purple. Periwinkles are blue," Sara told the child. "So are blue-eyed marys."

Stacy giggled. "Mary Blue-eyes. That's what I'm going to call her. Daddy, we named the kitten Mary Blue-eyes."

Cade went to the door. "An excellent name."

His heart went into overdrive. Sara was dressed in red shorts and a red-and-white top that left about six inches of her midriff bare. She had a little mole next to her navel. He remembered kissing it tenderly that weekend at the ranch.

Her eyes met his and the smile disappeared.

"I ordered a pizza," he said, pulling his tie off and freeing the upper button on his white shirt. "Would you like to join us while we get acquainted with Mary Blue-eyes?"

She shook her head. "Thanks, but I had a very late lunch."

''What did you do today?'' he asked, not sure he would like the answer.

''Researched records in Marin County.''

She stopped as if she'd said more than she meant to. He nodded and refrained from cross-examining her about the search. He knew it involved his father in some way, although he didn't know the details.

''Ah,'' he said, making a connection. ''The mysterious witness, perhaps?''

Her hands, holding the kitten securely in her lap, visibly jerked. The kitten gave a little meow. Stacy lifted it into her arms and nuzzled her face against its fur.

''I think Mary is hungry, Daddy,'' Stacy told him. ''Can I feed her now?''

''Yes. I left her stuff in the kitchen.'' After Stacy went inside with her new pet, Cade slung the tie over his shoulder and sat on the railing. ''What were you looking for in Marin County?'' he asked Sara.

''A bookstore.''

Her steady stare was defiant, which reminded him of his sister Jessica. If the two women joined forces, they would be a formidable pair.

''A bookstore.'' He mulled that over, but no clue about her reasons came to mind. ''I can help.''

She shook her head. ''I'm not busy.''

''You don't want my help?'' he goaded her a bit. ''I'm hurt. You and your fellow conspirators may not find what you're looking for.''

"We will." She lifted her chin and dared him to deny it.

Instead of becoming angry, he found himself staring at her lips and thinking of more intimate things.

"Don't," she said in a low voice.

"Don't think of kissing you? Or last weekend? Sorry, but I can't stop. You fill my head with the wildest images," he admitted. "I touch a flower and I'm reminded of your skin. Its softness. The silky smoothness of it."

"Shh," she hissed at him and glanced toward the door where Stacy had gone as if wishing the youngster would appear and save her from him.

He wanted to break through the shield she'd built between them. "I get a whiff of perfume and I remember all the fragrances of you. I can't forget the way you felt in my arms. I awake from a sound sleep because I think I've heard your laughter. Or your sigh. Tell me, teacher, how do I forget all that?"

"I don't know how we could have been so foolish," she whispered, desperation in her eyes.

He touched a finger to her temple. "At least you remember, too. I'm not suffering alone."

She turned her head to the side. "No, you're not alone, but Cade, we can't be lovers."

"Why not?" he demanded, wanting acquiescence, not arguments on what could never be. He wanted her soft and yielding in his arms, unable to resist the passion between them. He wanted the past, the future and all else to disappear so he could have her and this moment without worrying about consequences.

"Because," she said.

He looked into her eyes then, really looked, and saw the regret as well as the hunger. Triumph flickered within him, then was still.

"You're right. As long as the shadow of your father's death hangs over us, there's no place for other things."

"You don't think your father could have done it," she accused. "I saw it in your eyes last night."

"No, I don't. An accident, maybe, but murder, no."

"Before she died, my mother said he did. She said Walter had planned it and gave Jeremy something to make him pass out, then he threw him overboard."

Whatever the truth, Cade realized Sara believed her mother's story with all her heart. "Did you ever think that your mother may have been speaking from years of grief and resentment?"

"She was dying," Sara reminded him. "She had nothing to gain by then."

"Except to pass on her need for revenge for whatever wrongs she thought my father had committed against her children," he said softly. "You called him a seducer. Did you ever think it could be the other way—that your mother tried to seduce him and he rejected her?"

Like a door slamming, Sara hid all thoughts and feelings behind a solid mask. "It wasn't that way.

One thing I can say with certainty—Walter Parks didn't reject her.''

Cade studied her closed face. "What do you know that I don't?" he asked.

"Why don't you ask your father?" she suggested, her voice an accusing thread of sound against the traffic noises of the city.

He didn't tell her he already had and that Walter had denied any relationship. She went into her side of the duplex, her back stiff and forbidding, and closed the door.

Cade wondered exactly what her mother had told Sara and her siblings about his father. It was obvious Sara thought there had been an affair. He considered the situation. If Walter had been as attracted to his partner's wife as his son was to the daughter, then he felt damned sorry for his father. In either case, it was a no-win situation.

Chapter Ten

Sara noticed the Help Wanted sign in the window of the ice-cream shop when she went inside Friday afternoon. She was tired and discouraged. Since getting relieved of her job on Monday, she'd spent the week looking up business licenses in various towns and calling bookstores to see if anyone had ever heard of Derek Ross.

So far, no luck.

Mrs. Ling looked up from behind the counter where she was preparing an ice-cream soda. "Good afternoon," she said, smiling and nodding in her polite fashion. "Sara, isn't it?"

"Yes. I came in with Stacy the other day."

"How is she doing in school?"

"Fine." Sara glanced around. The usually pristine shop was messy. Tables needed busing and wiping clean. One family waited impatiently to place their order while Mrs. Ling served the couple ahead of them.

"It looks as if you've been busy," Sara commented. "Where's your help?"

"Yes, several people came in at once. Cyndi didn't show up. She called and said she couldn't work anymore. She stayed out late and her father is angry."

Sara made sympathetic noises, both for the teenager and the shop owner. "I'm free for the rest of the afternoon. Would you like a bit of help in getting caught up?"

Mrs. Ling gave her a relieved smile. "If you would be so good to do so, I would be pleased."

Sara went behind the counter and stashed her purse. "I used to work in a restaurant after school. This will be like old times."

Hard times, she thought to herself. The Carlton kids had always worked hard for spending money and new clothes.

She grabbed a towel from a sink filled with soapy bleach water, wrung it out and picked up a tray. In a few minutes, she had the tables clear and clean. She quickly washed and rinsed the dishes and put them in the drain rack to air dry. Mrs. Ling finished serving the family of four who'd been waiting behind the couple.

Mrs. Chong, the cat, snoozed on the windowsill in the sun. She had no worries.

For a second, Sara envied the easy life of the pet. "I noticed the Help Wanted sign. Had any takers?"

Mrs. Ling was obviously surprised. "Not yet. It's part-time, from two until six. Do you know someone?"

"Me. My class was canceled, so I'm at loose ends. A part-time job would fit my schedule just fine." Sara smiled brightly and waited for the store owner to decide. Feeling warmth around her ankles, she leaned down and scratched the cat's ears. "Hey, Mrs. Chong, how are you?"

"Mrs. Chong and I would love to have you in the shop," Mrs. Ling said. "Can you start Monday? I have a high-school girl who comes in on weekends."

"Great. I'll see you then. In the meantime, I'll take two scoops of the mint chocolate chip ice cream."

"An excellent choice," the shopkeeper told her.

At her feet, Mrs. Chong purred loudly and wove her body around Sara's ankles. At least someone wanted her, Sara thought, trying not to feel sorry for herself.

By the time she reached the town house, she'd finished the treat. It was early afternoon, so she sat on the deck and tried to read, but magazine articles didn't hold her attention. They seemed superficial and falsely cheerful.

Just the way she felt.

She tried to smile, but her lips wouldn't cooperate.

She hadn't been this dispirited since the cold, dark days of last winter. It was still winter in her heart, she mused.

When Tyler called and asked her to meet him on his dinner break, she agreed at once. At six o'clock, she walked to their favorite Chinese restaurant. Her brother was waiting for her, looking very handsome in a new summer suit.

"Why aren't girls falling all over you?" she demanded. "Or are they and you aren't talking?"

He flashed her a grin. "I don't have time to mess with girls." He became serious once they were seated. "How did you do today?"

She recounted her research efforts. "I called every bookstore from San Leandro to Richmond and asked if they knew Derek Ross or something like that."

"No luck?"

"None." She sighed.

"Mark is checking each neighborhood he goes to while on other jobs, so it isn't costing us anything."

"He's nice."

"Yeah. Too bad you didn't fall for him instead of Cade Parks."

Sara's insides felt like taffy being pulled slowly apart. "I didn't fall for Cade."

"You can fool yourself," Tyler said, "but don't try to fool your big brother."

"You're my little brother."

"I'm bigger than you are," he reminded her. "I'm sorry, sis, that I brought you into this."

"I came here with my eyes open. I knew what I was doing." She shrugged and rubbed the moisture off the side of the water glass. "Has Cade spoken to you?"

"No, but I'm sure he's determined to get involved. He said he wants to know the truth as much as we do. Huh," Tyler said with a snort to express his doubts.

She nodded. "That's what he told me. He thinks we're wrong, though, about his father's guilt. He wants to be involved in order to prove Walter's innocence."

Tyler shrugged. "I suppose I would, too, if it were my father—" He stopped abruptly, his gaze locking with hers. "Hell, his father *is* my father. It's too awful to think about," he ended in disgust.

"A very tangled web," Sara said, thinking of Cade and his daughter. "Stacy is so young, only a year older than I was when we left California."

Tyler's expression softened a bit. "She's a bright kid. Really cute."

"And loving," Sara added. "She's very trusting of those she loves."

"Yeah. If only it was as simple for adults," he said with an undercurrent of bitterness in the words.

Sara wondered if he was thinking of the woman, the "one-night stand" who had intrigued him so. She thought of the future, which seemed dismal for each of them, then murmured, "It's ironic, isn't it?"

"What is?"

"That we had to come to San Francisco to discover our true loves? It's like we had to return to the place of our origins in order to find what we really wanted."

"I was born in Denver," Tyler reminded her.

"But you were conceived here," she said softly. "You and Conrad were the two good things that came from that tragic period. I adored you both the moment you were born." Her smile was nostalgic.

Tyler squeezed her hand. "Poor sis," he mocked, but in a gentle tone. "Your loves have all been a disappointment."

"Not you," she immediately assured him. She summoned a smile. "You're the best of the bunch."

He shook his head. "Maybe Cade is," he suggested. "Of all Walter Parks's children, including me and Conrad, I think perhaps Cade is the most idealistic. I have a gut feeling we can trust him."

Sara stared into her brother's eyes. He returned her gaze levelly. "He thinks Walter is innocent," she murmured. "He won't help us prove otherwise."

"But he'll accept the truth if we can find it. I don't think he'll let his father sweep anything under the carpet." Tyler hesitated, then said, "I'm going for a DNA test in a couple of weeks. We need a sample from Walter. Maybe Cade could get it for us."

Sara was horrified. "We can't ask him to do that. It would be a…a betrayal of his family."

"Okay, it was just a thought."

"Well, don't think like that." Looking into her

brother's knowing eyes, Sara realized the impact of her heated reprimand. "I won't involve him in the downfall of his father," she said. "He already has reason enough to despise us."

Tyler nodded, his gaze sympathetic, as if he could see into her heart and knew of the turmoil there.

Cade paused beside his car and warily studied the man who was studying him. He'd already had a full day at the office. He didn't need more things to think about at the present, thanks just the same.

However, it looked as if his day wasn't over yet.

"Got time for a cup of coffee?" Tyler Carlton asked.

Cade shrugged. "Am I under arrest or is this merely a friendly inquisition?"

"I'm on my own time right now," the younger man said.

Cade looked at the coffee shop across the street. For a Friday evening, the place wasn't all that busy. "That okay?"

"Yeah."

He and the detective waited for the light on the corner, then crossed the noisy street and went into the comparatively quiet restaurant. The waiter brought them water and menus as soon as they were seated. A couple of minutes later, he was back, pen in hand. Both ordered coffee.

"This is the best service I've ever gotten here,"

Cade remarked sardonically. "You come here often?"

"Yeah."

Again Cade was aware of the other man's keen perusal. "To what do I owe the honor of this visit?"

"Sara."

A quick jolt flew along Cade's nerves. "What about her?" he asked, guarding against any telltale emotion.

"I think she's in love with you. What do you think?"

"That she's trying to prove my father guilty of murder," Cade spoke quietly, so his voice didn't carry to an arguing couple three tables from them.

"Right," the brother agreed. "That's why we moved back here. Meeting you has complicated things for her in a way I didn't expect." He heaved a sigh. "Life has a way of playing mean tricks on a person."

"Tell me about it," Cade muttered.

"The question I need answered is, how do you feel about her?"

Cade decided not to tell Sara's kin where to get off, but he wasn't sure how much he wanted to confess. "I have a question." When Tyler nodded, Cade continued, "Why did she go to the ranch with me?"

"I told her to," Tyler said promptly. "I thought she could maybe pry some information out of you about your family's finances, where the money came from and that sort of thing."

Cade felt a sinking inside, sort of like stepping into an elevator, then discovering it wasn't there. "Yeah, she asked questions."

"I think it went further than talk," Tyler told him, his eyes—green like Sara's—boring holes through him.

"Ask your sister," Cade advised.

"I'm asking you."

Cade met the hard stare with one of his own. Between the Carltons and his father, he'd spent the week questioning every aspect of his life. It didn't look as if the weekend was going to be an improvement.

"There are feelings," he said candidly, "but as long as she thinks my father killed hers, I don't see a future."

"Do you really want to find out the truth?"

"Yes." Cade didn't blink while the lawman gave him another once-over. He waited it out.

"Okay," Tyler said. "Here's our side of the story."

Cade listened without interrupting as the tale of greed and diamond-smuggling and murder unfolded. "That's a pretty sordid story," he said at the end.

Tyler nodded. "There's plenty of sin to spread around."

"None as great as my father's. If what you say is true. You'll have to find this uncle to prove it." Cade frowned. "Even then it'll be his word against my father's. Having kept silent all these years, your uncle will be under as much suspicion as the old man."

"Does your mother know the truth?"

Cade couldn't hide his surprise at the question. "I don't think so. I read the police reports. The housekeeper said my mother had already returned home when the yacht went back out to sea that night."

"Yeah, I read the reports, too."

"I don't think she had reason to lie." Cade paused and considered. Mrs. Wheeler, newly widowed at the time, had just started her job with his family. He couldn't imagine her lying for anyone for any reason.

"There are other...difficulties," Tyler said after a brief silence. "I can't tell you about them now, but I can assure you all will come to light soon."

A chill raced along his neck. Cade rubbed the spot, then heaved a deep breath. "I'm angry with Sara. She used me and Stace for her own purposes, but I don't want her hurt."

"If it's any comfort, it was troublesome to her. She doesn't like for children to be involved. You still willing to help with the investigation?"

Cade considered what he owed his father, himself and the woman who'd breached his defenses. "I'm willing to discover the truth."

"But are you willing to disclose it once it's found?"

"Yes," Cade said grimly. "What do you know of this uncle?"

Sara opened the back door like a thief in the night. She'd stayed hidden inside since returning home from the meeting with Tyler, ignoring Stacy's call to "come play with me and Mary Blue-eyes" earlier in the evening. With Tai back on the job, Sara thought it best to avoid the family next door as much as possible.

Night had fallen, so she should be safe out on the deck at this hour. It was after ten o'clock. Glancing up, she saw a light on in Cade's bedroom. He was probably reading some legal documents or something.

She sank into the cushions of a deck chair and propped her bare feet on the railing. The night was unusually warm, and she could see thousands of stars in the sky. Not as many as she'd seen at the ranch last weekend, but...

Images immediately danced across her inner vision. Riding a horse. Washing a cow's teats. Making love so passionately it had stolen her breath away. The contentment afterward and a sense of rightness had been a gift.

A door opened behind her. Tension invaded every cell of her body. It could only be one person.

"Enjoying the night air?" Cade asked. He pulled a chair away from the table, took a seat and, like her, propped his sock-clad feet on the deck railing.

"Yes."

"Would you rather be alone?"

No. Yes.

The answers warred within her. She shrugged, unable to decide between them.

"I saw Tyler this evening."

She was startled. "When?"

"When I left the office, he was waiting for me. We had a long talk over coffee. I know about the missing uncle."

"Oh." Her thoughts went every which way. Tyler must have gone directly to Cade after leaving her. Had he mentioned the paternity issue?

Glancing at Cade's relaxed pose, she decided her brother was keeping that little secret to himself for the time being. It certainly wasn't her news to confide.

"I also had a talk with my father this morning."

She tensed, waiting for an accusation, a denial, something out of the ordinary.

"He admitted he spoke to one of the other directors about you. I'm sorry for that."

Relief washed over her. "Then it wasn't you."

"No." He paused. "I would never willingly do anything to hurt you. I think you've had enough of that in your life."

"Sometimes I think it will never be over."

"I hope that isn't true."

They sat there in silence, but it suddenly wasn't uncomfortable to her. A warm foot touched hers. Cade angled his toes to fit under hers and stroked the underside of her foot. Tingles ran from the spot all the way up her leg.

Her insides, which seemed made of gelatin, quivered deliciously. She wanted him. In spite of everything, including common sense, she wanted him more than she wanted her next breath.

"Let's forget everything and pretend we just met for the first time a few minutes ago," he said.

"Ha," she said softly.

"I didn't say it wouldn't be hard. Would it be impossible?" he asked.

She had only to recall the weekend at his ranch to know it would be all too easy to let herself be tugged into the sweet tide of bliss with him. "No," she whispered. "Not impossible, but—"

"Shhh," he said. "My name is Cade. What's yours?"

"Sara," she replied after a moment.

"Hello, Sara," he murmured in a voice that was husky and intimate and sexy. "Nice night, huh?"

"I can't do this," she protested, pressing her hands to her eyes. "I can't pretend."

Before she knew what was happening, she was lifted from the chair. Cade carried her inside her town house and gently laid her on the leather sofa. "You can. Whatever problems the week holds, let's keep the weekend to ourselves."

He sat beside her and smoothed the hair from her temples, then massaged her there. "Do you have a headache?"

"Not now. I did earlier."

"You think too much."

His chuckle did things to her insides. "There's so much to think about."

"This?" he suggested, rubbing a finger over her

lips and making them tingle with anticipation. "This?"

Cupping her breasts, he traced circles over them with his thumbs. His eyes never left hers. In the dim light, she felt they were isolated from all else, two people alone in their own world for these precious moments.

"I can't think at all when you do that," she admitted on a breathless gasp.

"Good." He bent forward and kissed her very, very tenderly. "We don't need to think to enjoy this."

She discovered that was true. As long as they kissed, as long as their hands busily caressed each other in pleasure, there was no need to think about tomorrow.

Somehow clothing slipped out of the way, taking problems and inhibitions with it. His long warm body covered hers, and for an eternity known only to them, they existed as one heart, one soul.

"So beautiful," he murmured. "Each time I hold you, it gets better and better."

"Yes, oh, yes." She pressed frantic kisses along his throat, little bites of ecstasy on his shoulder.

He licked her breasts, laid a trail of hot kisses down the middle of her body, explored all her erotic spots until she writhed and twisted under him, wanting more and more and more...

"Cade," she whispered. "Oh, love, come to me."

He took care of protection, then followed her bidding, unable to resist the hunger that rode them both.

He brought her to fulfillment once, let her rest, then started the journey all over again, never wanting it to end.

At last the need became too great. Bliss exploded inside him, sending shattering sensation to every nerve until the world disappeared. There was only the two of them. He thrust deeply, wanting time to stand still, wanting the moment to last forever.

Only later, lying in heated contentment while still pressed tightly together, did reality return.

Cade stiffened at a slight snuffling sound, then Stacy's voice penetrated the dark. "Mary Blue-eyes," his daughter sang out.

Beside him, Sara went rigid.

"It's okay," he murmured. "She talks in her sleep."

They listened, but no more sounds came from the monitor he'd left on, tucked into his jeans pocket.

"She's such a darling," Sara said, relaxing against him once more. "I wish…"

"What?"

"I wish she were mine."

She opened her eyes and gazed at him. His heart did a flip. "So do I. I wish she were ours."

He kissed away the tears she couldn't hide and felt a spark of hope. There had to be a way for this to work. Worry returned. It all depended on the past, he thought, and how it was finally resolved.

Chapter Eleven

Sara sat on the deck after breakfast and read the Saturday morning paper. Cade was there, too. They'd spent the night on the sofa, then awakened early. After each had showered and dressed in their own town house, Sara had prepared eggs and toast. They'd eaten outside while waiting for Stacy to wake.

"Well, look who's up," Cade said when the child made her appearance, still in her pajamas. She carried the kitten tucked up against her shoulder. "Did you and Mary Blue-eyes have a good night?"

"Yes," Stacy told him. "We're hungry."

Sara said hello to Stacy and petted the kitten, while Cade went inside to prepare cereal for the girl and kitty food for Mary.

"Let's go to the ranch and ride today," Stacy said after eating. She sat on the deck and rolled a ball for Mary, who chased it zealously.

"Good idea," Cade said.

"You two go," Sara told them. "You need some family time together."

"But we want you," Stacy immediately stated her opinion. "Don't we, Daddy?"

"We certainly do."

Cade gave her a lazy grin, looking so handsome, Sara's heart went all soft. "I should do some work," she said, but not very convincingly.

"It's Saturday. The courthouses and city records offices are closed. All work and no play will make Sara a dull girl," he warned.

"So you have to go with us," Stacy said.

Looking at their smiling faces, Sara found she really had no choice. For the first time in her life, she felt truly wanted for herself, for the simple pleasure of her company, with no other designs or demands on her. It was, quite simply, wonderful.

"Will we spend the night?" she asked.

"Yes," Cade answered. "We'll return early tomorrow afternoon. Stace and I will have dinner with my father."

Stacy wrinkled her nose. "We went there last time. Grandpa's not much fun."

"Stace," Cade said in a warning tone.

"Well, he's not. But I won't tell him," she promised her father, her expression one of great earnestness. "We don't want to hurt his feelings," she explained to Sara.

Sara was touched by the girl's sincerity and concern for others. Stacy was successfully making the journey from a young child's subjective view of the world to one that included others and their feelings. The girl could be hurt by her and Cade if they weren't careful.

"Let's go," Cade said, breaking into her worried thoughts. "Meet us at the front door in, um, fifteen minutes?"

"Yea-a-a," Stacy shouted. "Last one ready is a really, really rotten egg."

Sara nodded and hurried inside to grab a change of clothing and a toothbrush, feeling as excited as a kid playing hooky. She laughed as she packed her few items, picked up her purse and jacket and rushed to be the first one at the door.

Stacy was already there, her pink pull-along case beside her. "I beat you and Daddy."

"Did you pack your toothbrush?" Sara asked with a mock ferocious frown. "Pajamas? A change of clothes?"

"I did everything," the child declared.

"Let's get out of Dodge," Cade said, coming out on the stoop and locking the door. They raced to the car and soon joined the line of traffic on the Golden Gate Bridge, each vehicle heading out of town, the occupants on their own adventures.

* * *

Cade reluctantly entered his father's house Sunday evening. He headed for the library while Stacy ran to the kitchen to report on the kitten's progress to Mrs. Wheeler.

"Good evening, Father," he said, finding the older man striding up and down the space between the window and the rich simplicity of the mahogany desk.

Walter stopped pacing and gave Cade a calculating perusal. Cade was startled at his appearance. The old man looked as if he hadn't slept during the intervening week. "You okay?" Cade asked.

Walter dismissed the question with a jerk of his hand. Reaching into his pocket, he pulled out a device hardly larger than a hearing-aid battery and thrust it toward Cade.

Cade took the item and studied it. "What is it?"

"A wiretapping device," Walter informed him, a definite snarl on his lips. "Someone tapped my office phone."

"How? I thought your secretary guarded the inner sanctum more closely than the guards at Buckingham Palace guard the queen."

"I don't know how, but I know who."

Cade observed his father's anger dispassionately. He'd been through scenes with the old man so often, it no longer fazed him, although Rowan was usually the brunt of the fury.

"Who?" Cade asked.

"Your new friends. Sara Carlton and her brother. Their friends, the Banning brothers."

A cold hand reached inside Cade and sent icicles deep into his gut. "What makes you think that?"

"More than one can play this game," Walter said, his eyes narrowed craftily. "I decided to investigate them and hired my own detective. They're snooping into my business. That's an invasion of privacy, if nothing else."

"Did you report this to the police?" Cade asked, nodding toward the tiny snooping device. "It should have been checked for fingerprints before anyone handled it."

"Not yet. I need more evidence." Walter lifted the transmitter from Cade's hand, put it in an envelope and placed it in the top drawer of the desk. His eyes gleamed as if already witnessing a victory over Sara and her group of comrades-in-arms. "When I get it, they'll be sorry."

Cade had never seen his father look so sinister. But then, the man had a right to be furious. Listening to a person's private conversations was against the law. Even the FBI couldn't ordinarily do it without a judge's okay.

Some part of him didn't want to believe Sara had anything to do with it, but standing back and studying the situation objectively, he admitted she and her brother were the prime suspects, even though Mark Banning might have done the actual deed.

"There's one other thing," Cade said, recalling his own anger with his father. "I want you to call the chairman of the board for Stacy's school and have Sara reinstated.''

"It'll be a cold day in hell before I'll do anything for a Carlton.''

"Your action was unfair and unfounded,'' Cade continued.

"What about the wiretap?'' Walter demanded.

"Like you said, you need more evidence. You don't really know who planted it. Whatever case Sara and her brother think they have against you, it has nothing to do with their careers. Sara, by all accounts, is an excellent teacher. She doesn't deserve to have her professional reputation sullied by lies and innuendo.''

"I didn't lie,'' Walter said, his eyes narrowing dangerously as he stared at Cade as if daring him to pursue the topic.

Cade took a deep breath and ignored the warning in his father's harsh expression. "If you don't, I'll call and tell him you got Sara confused with a family you knew long ago and that you were mistaken about her.''

"You wouldn't dare,'' Walter said in a savage tone.

"I can promise you I will. First thing in the morning,'' he added, carefully maintaining an even tone.

His brother had called their father a spider, weaving people into his web until he controlled every aspect of their lives. Cade thought of his position at the law firm, the ranch that he and Stacy loved, the family loyalty that he'd accepted as natural.

He sensed the silky strands wrapping around him, luring him into a lifetime of captivity so that each decision he dared make on his own would be more and more of a struggle. In such a situation, when did a person give in and give up?

"Call him," Cade said again, harder this time.

The telltale vein that acted as a gauge to his father's temper throbbed violently. "A mistake," Walter murmured. "I can admit to a mistake."

"First thing in the morning."

His father smiled. Alarm bells went off in Cade's mind, but he couldn't tell what the old man was thinking.

"Yes. All right. Here're the girls," Walter said, hearing their voices in the hallway. "This discussion is between you and me."

Cade nodded. He saw no need to involve his sisters in the mess.

Emily and Jessica entered the library, each wearing identical worried expressions. "Rowan is gone," Jessica said, her accusing eyes going to their father.

"What do you mean gone?" Walter snapped at her.

Emily stepped between the other two. "He apparently hasn't been at his house all week. He doesn't answer the phone or return messages. The mail hasn't been taken in. Jessica and I went over today. His neighbors haven't seen him since last Sunday. He briefly returned home after the dinner over here, then left 'in a cloud of smoke' was the way the old man across the street put it.''

Cade wasn't surprised. His younger brother had been furious with their father when he'd left. He felt his own anger as a cold, churning sea within him. The question was, who deserved it—his father for disillusioning him, or Sara for using him?

Logic forced him to agree with Walter's conclusion. The Carltons were the most likely ones to have his father's office bugged. Recalling the questions she'd asked him about his family, he felt like a fool for thinking there was an innocence and fragility about her.

But fair was fair, his conscience prodded. Her quest for revenge against his family had nothing to do with her abilities as a teacher.

The meal was long and boring, in Cade's estimation. He steeled himself to patience and got through it and the undercurrents of hostility that undercut the carefully polite conversation around the dinner table. At last he collected Stacy and left.

After the bath-and-story ritual, Cade rubbed his daughter's back while she drifted easily into sleep. For her, the world centered on her new kitten and her friends at kindergarten. If only life were that simple.

A little after nine o'clock, he stepped out onto the back deck. The wind was too cool to be outside, and he found the chairs empty. He knocked softly on Sara's door.

She answered at once. "Hello. I heard you and Stacy come home earlier."

Her smile was open and friendly. She seemed so damned sincere. He shook his head, denying his own need to believe she was as innocent as she appeared.

"Cade, what is it?" she asked, picking up on the angry vibes that strummed through him.

"I'll ask the questions," he told her, hardening himself to the task.

"What questions?" She blinked her cat-green eyes and stared up at him.

"Did you and your brother have a wiretap planted in my father's office?"

Her mouth dropped open. If it was an act of complete surprise, it was a good one. She shook her head.

"Someone evidently did. My father found the bug. Should I check my phone at the law office and see if it's been tapped, too?"

Her expression closed like a curtain coming down on the last act of a bad play. "I don't know about your family, but mine doesn't operate that way."

"Perhaps you should check with your brother and his friends," Cade suggested.

She picked up the phone and punched in a number, her eyes never leaving him. "Tyler? Did you have Walter Parks's telephone bugged?"

Cade heard the brother's expletive, then denial. The anger lessened fractionally.

"Did Nick or Mark do it?" Sara asked. Another denial. "Good. That's all I wanted to know."

The brother talked some more, but Cade couldn't hear the words since he'd lowered his voice considerably.

"Cade is here. He seems to think we had his father's phone tapped. Also his at his office. Thanks. I'll talk to you later. No, don't come over. It isn't necessary. Bye for now." She hung up, then looked his way. "We're in the clear. Perhaps your father should check out the people he has business dealings with. He apparently has more than one set of enemies."

A battle raged inside Cade as he studied the woman who gazed back at him with ice in her eyes, her chin tilted at an indignant angle. "I want to believe you," he said. He gave a snort of laughter. "Even now, I want to believe you."

A hint of hopelessness surrounded her as she shrugged. "That's a decision I can't help you with."

He locked his gaze with hers. "Who else should I suspect, Sara?" he demanded softly, knowing the question was futile. "No one else has accused my father of murder."

She didn't turn away from the probing stare he sent her way. He'd known another woman who could look him straight in the eye and lie without a qualm. His wife had perfected the picture of injured innocence long ago. Sara wasn't nearly as good at appearing the fragile heroine.

"We'll prove it," she said, her voice low. "It may

be the last thing Tyler and I do, but we'll prove it. And we'll stay within the law while we do, Cade.''

"Unlike my family," he added, finishing her unspoken thought.

"You said it, not me."

He pressed the fingers of one hand to his forehead where a pounding ache had settled just above his eyes. He wanted to believe Sara, but that would mean he had to disbelieve the family patriarch.

Why would his father lie?

To discredit the Carltons, the answer came to him.

Yes, but would he pretend the bug had been planted in his office? The old man had produced the device as evidence. Cade doubted his father knew where to get such things.

There were ways to find out…such as from a private detective, that insidious part of him answered.

"Please leave," Sara said, interrupting the internal argument. "Don't…don't come back. Not ever."

"I have to. I have to get to the bottom of this, otherwise we have no future—"

"I think we can safely rule that out."

The finality of her statement was obvious. "Think what you want," he told her, "but until the past is resolved, we are involved." He walked to the door and paused. "In more ways than one."

Because, God help him, he still wanted her and all that they had shared over the weekend, he admitted, going to his own place and grimly locking the door behind him as if by doing so he could lock her out of his mind.

And his heart?

Next time, he vowed, he would know the truth, the whole truth and nothing but the truth before he let himself be a fool for a woman again.

Sara stared at the calendar the next morning. It was Monday, the last week of July. She'd been in town for nearly a month. Nothing was going the way she'd planned.

Such as falling in love?

She certainly hadn't planned on doing anything as foolish as that. She still couldn't believe Cade had accused her and Tyler of bugging his father's office.

But maybe they should have. Maybe then they could find out what the conniving Parks family was up to.

At the ring of the doorbell, she stopped the tortured thoughts and went to answer. Tyler stood there looking handsome and older than his years in a conservative suit.

"Was I expecting you?" she asked. "I didn't prepare breakfast. I'm out of eggs."

"Borrow some from your neighbor." He came inside, bringing the freshness of the morning with him. The sun was already breaking through the low clouds, promising a hot day to come.

"I don't think so." She managed a tongue-in-cheek amusement that he didn't fall for.

He patted her shoulder and asked if she had any coffee. They served themselves and went into the den. "Where are you going this morning?" he asked.

"Oakland. I'm checking the bookstores there today." She paused to consider. "I've been calling independent bookstores, but what if Derek Ross sold out and works for a chain now? Maybe he's a manager at Barnes & Noble or Waldenbooks or someplace like that."

"Let's stick with the independents for now. Tell me everything that Cade said to you last night about this phone-tapping episode."

Sara recounted the brief conversation.

"So he actually saw the transmitter?" Tyler asked.

"I think so. That's what I assumed."

Tyler frowned mightily. "This could get complicated if someone else is investigating Parks. I need to talk to Cade."

Sara stared at her brother. "Why, for heaven's sake?"

Tyler studied her for a few seconds. "I think he wants to get at the truth. He'll help us find out what we need to know."

"You're wrong. He's furious about the wiretap. His first thought was that we did the dirty deed."

"That's what I would think, too," Tyler agreed. He gave her a wry grin. "If he's investigating us and we're investigating him, then we may as well work together."

"You're insane."

"Yeah, but trust me on this one. The son isn't privy to the father's sins. Cade is probably going through hell right now. I can identify with that."

"Great," she snapped. "You and he can commiserate together, but leave me out of it."

"It smarts when the person you love doesn't trust you, doesn't it?" he asked on a philosophical note.

Emotion flashed through his eyes and was gone, hidden behind his usual devil-may-care attitude. Sara was at once sympathetic. "Is that the way you feel, Tyler?"

His smile was insouciant. "Nah, no love lost here. It's you I'm talking about."

She lifted her chin. "I'm not in love, either."

Her brother headed for the front of the duplex. "I've got to get to the station." He stopped before opening the door. "Don't let our mother's bitterness blind you to the good things in life when they come along."

Sara nodded, bid him goodbye, then lingered at the open door until he'd driven out of sight. His manner surprised her. He seemed to be on Cade's side in this argument. He apparently *trusted* her handsome neighbor.

She didn't. During the long hours of the night, she'd thought about her mother's affair with Cade's father. Before meeting Cade she'd found that difficult to comprehend, but now, well, she could understand Marla's fascination with Walter Parks. As a young man, he'd probably been as handsome and beguiling as his son.

Crossing her arms tightly over her middle, Sara returned to the den and picked up the map of Oakland. She had work to do this morning.

"Good afternoon, Sara," Mrs. Ling greeted her at two o'clock when she arrived for work.

"Hello. You're busy. I'd better get to work."

The tiny ice-cream parlor was crowded. Sara donned an apron to protect her red pantsuit and started busing tables right away. Once those were clean, she went behind the counter and scooped ice cream onto waffle or plain cones while Mrs. Ling handled drinks and the cash register. They didn't have a breather until almost six o'clock.

"I didn't realize so many people liked ice cream," she said, wiggling her toes in her loafers. "My feet are so tired, they're numb."

Mrs. Ling pointed to her own footgear. "I wear jogging shoes. You should, too."

The shop mascot jumped daintily down from the window sill and came over to rub around Sara's ankles. "Do you feel sorry for me, Mrs. Chong?" she asked, stooping to give the cat a scratch behind the ears.

Mrs. Chong purred loudly.

"She does," Sara said with a smile.

The door opened. "Hi, Sara," Stacy called out. "Hi, Mrs. Ling and Mrs. Chong."

The girl's father followed her into the shop. His glance took in her apron and the cleaning cloth in her hand. "You're working here?" he asked, a frown gathering in his eyes.

"Neat," Stacy said in approval at Sara's nod. "You can eat all the ice cream you want, huh?"

Sara managed to compose her face into a serene smile, although she could do nothing about her heart and its frantic beating. "What can I get for you?"

"We have strawberries and little round cakes for dessert," Stacy informed her, "so we want vanilla ice cream to go with it. Do you want to eat with us?"

"Uh, thanks, but not tonight," Sara replied. She glanced at Cade. "A pint of vanilla?" she asked.

He nodded.

She was acutely aware of him as she scooped ice cream into a pint box. He'd swapped his work suit for khakis, T-shirt, sneakers and a baseball cap. The casual attire made him look much more approachable, as if he belonged to her world rather than that of Parks Fine Jewelry. And she was crazy to be thinking like that.

After putting the ice-cream container in a plastic bag, she handed it to Stacy, then took his money, counted out the change and handed it to him.

"What time do you get off?" he asked.

For some reason, she was reluctant to tell him. "Six," she finally said. Her eyes went to the wall clock when his did. She had five more minutes.

"We'll wait and walk you home," he said.

She shook her head. "I'm going to stop at the noodle shop and eat first."

Stacy straightened up from rubbing Mrs. Chong. "Eat with us, Sara. We're fixing chicken and we made enough for you, too."

Before she could politely refuse, Cade spoke up. "Stace is right. We'll have plenty. I need to talk to you."

Seeing no graceful way out, Sara nodded.

"Go," Mrs. Ling said, making sweeping motions with her hands. "You've worked hard today. My son will come by and help me until closing."

Sara removed her apron, folded it and placed it under the counter where she'd left her purse. Putting the purse strap over her shoulder, she said good-night to the shop owner and left with Cade and Stacy. Fortunately, the girl kept up a steady stream of chatter all the way home.

At the house, Sara insisted on making a salad to contribute to the meal and heated crunchy sourdough rolls while Cade grilled chicken kabobs with chunks of pineapple, onions and mushrooms on the back deck. Shortly before seven o'clock, they sat at the patio table and ate while Mary Blue-eyes chased a butterfly in the tiny backyard.

"Now we get to watch a video," Stacy announced. "It's the Muppets."

"You can watch it," Cade interceded. "Sara and I are going to sit out here and watch the sunset. Take the kitten inside with you."

"Okay." The girl bounced inside with her pet after her father nodded.

"More iced tea, or would you prefer wine? I have a Chablis in the refrigerator."

"Iced tea, please," Sara requested. She wanted to keep an absolutely clear head in any discussion with Cade.

He carried their dishes into the town house and returned in a few minutes with tea for her and a glass of white wine for himself.

Sara observed him in quick, surreptitious glances while sipping her drink. He still made her heart pound, she admitted. He had a clean-cut openness that made her want to trust him. She wanted to confide all the secrets about her family and his and ask his advice.

But she didn't dare let herself trust him that much. He obviously felt the same about her. She sighed. "What did you want to talk to me about?"

"I spoke to my father about your position at Lakeside," he said, taking his seat, his eyes dark and moody as he gazed at her. "He called the chairman of the board and explained he'd mixed you up with a family he knew a long time ago. You can return to the teaching position tomorrow."

"I told Mrs. Ling I would work from two until six during the week," Sara told him.

He shrugged. "It's up to you. Personally, I wouldn't blame you for not going back to Lakeside. You were dismissed without just cause."

She tried to read his thoughts, but his face disclosed nothing. "I don't know how you did it, but thank you for…for straightening this out."

He nodded without saying anything, giving her the impression that he'd said all he intended about the subject.

"Did you have words with your father about this?" she asked.

A cynical smile brushed his lips briefly. "What do you think?" Before she could reply, he continued, "What does it matter? You're reinstated, so that's the end of it."

Not quite, she wanted to tell him. More than ever, she wanted to show the world what kind of scoundrel Walter Parks really was. The more she knew of him, the more she thought him capable of instigating evil.

Looking at the son, who shared so many of his father's physical characteristics, she wished Cade wasn't related to her enemy. "I don't think you're like your father," she said. "I don't blame you for his sins."

"Such as murder?" Cade inquired. "Thanks. That's a real comfort to know."

She stood. "I'm sorry. I'm sorry for everything."

"Does that mean you'll back off on investigating my father for your father's death?"

Sara shook her head. "No. I can't. My mother loved my father. She was unhappy and confused at the time of the…the incident, but she never thought of losing him. It hurt her so."

Cade listened, his eyes never leaving her. When she finished, he nodded as if he understood. "Well, then, as they say, I'll see you in court…when you prove your case. If you do."

"We will."

She went inside and closed the door. Cade continued to sit on the deck, his eyes turned toward the far horizon as if he sought some truth or ancient wisdom there.

Following his gaze, she noticed the sun had almost disappeared. Only a sliver was visible. She waited, her whole being suspended in the moment, then the sun slipped below the sea.

There was no green flash.

Chapter Twelve

"Don't look so worried," a feminine voice advised. "It can't be that bad."

Cade, lost in introspection, turned to his sister. "Hey, Em," he greeted her. "It's too lovely a day to be worried about anything. You look like a million bucks."

She was dressed in a summer suit of soft pink with touches of green that enhanced her golden-brown hair and green eyes. Her dimples flashed when she smiled at him.

The hostess summoned them at that moment, and they followed her to a table. After they were seated and had given their orders for drinks, he studied his twin.

"What? Do I have a smudge on my nose?" she asked.

He shook his head. "I was thinking about time and how it slips away on a person. Do you realize we're going to be thirty, come November?"

"It's too awful to contemplate." Her grin belied the complaint in the words.

Like the sunrise, his twin had been one of the constants in his life. Em and Wheelie. Affection for the two women eased the gloom that had sat on his shoulders for the past two days.

"What is it?" she demanded, narrowing her eyes as she returned his perusal.

She'd always been good at grasping his moods, he realized. Of the four Parks kids, she was the most sensitive and concerned for others. "Why hasn't some man eloped with you yet?"

Her smile faltered and emotion flickered through her eyes for a second before she clasped her hands to her breast and gazed into the distance with a dreamy expression. "I'm waiting for my prince to come."

"Huh. I'm not sure there are any of those around anymore, Sleeping Beauty."

"Then I'll be what I am—a spinster who plans other people's weddings while secretly pining for my own." She tilted her head slightly. "What about you? Stacy needs a brother or sister, and you're not getting any younger."

"Don't remind me."

They placed their luncheon order, then observed the flow of diners in and out of the busy bistro.

"What's with our dear father these days?" Emily asked after a bit. "He usually ignores me and Jessica. Now all of a sudden he's realized we're alive. Two Sunday dinner invitations in a row. He's worried about something." She frowned as she lifted a glass of raspberry tea and took a sip. "Something serious," she added.

"It appears he thinks someone is out to get him or something like that."

"Mmm, makes one wonder what he's got to hide."

Looking into her candid gaze, Cade knew Em didn't have a clue how serious the situation actually was. A murderer could still be brought to trial twenty-five years after the deed. Appalled, he realized he was beginning to think like Sara.

As usual, his body reacted to the merest thought of her. No matter what his mind dictated, physically he was attuned to her. Odder still was the fact that something in him insisted on trusting her and her brother. He couldn't quite discount their story and their drive to discover the truth behind it. He exhaled in frustration.

"Cade, are you in love?" Emily asked, breaking into his introspection.

He found he couldn't answer the question. "Why do you ask that?"

"Stacy mentioned that your neighbor had gone to

the ranch with you. I've never known you to take any woman to your secret hideaway.''

''So you think it has to mean something?''

''Yes.''

She smiled when he glared at her, giving him a glimpse of the young happy person she used to be. The way they both had been once upon a time.

''Damn,'' he said.

Emily burst into laughter. ''You are. Cade's in love, Cade's in love,'' she said in a singsong, but softly so the nearby diners couldn't hear.

It was almost a relief to bring it out into the open, he found. ''Father will disown me if I join forces with the Carltons,'' he said ruefully.

''Do you care? You're an adult, a successful attorney. Do what you want, what your heart tells you is right.''

''You sound like Jessica. Or Rowan.''

Her teasing manner disappeared. ''I'm worried about him. He's totally disappeared. Jessica and I call everyday. No answer. I stopped by and collected his mail this morning. I hope no burglars have noticed the house is empty. This is so like him,'' she concluded in annoyance.

''He can take care of himself. It's Jessica I'm worried about. She and Rowan never knew much of a family life. She was, what, a year old when Mother was sent away?''

Emily nodded. ''We had Wheelie. And you. You

were always a wonderful brother. You deserve someone who loves you with all her heart.''

"So do you, Em. The men in this town must be stupid.''

She looked troubled. "I have a…a doomsday sense of time passing. If we don't grab happiness when it sails by, we may never have another chance. Don't let that happen to you. If this Sara Carlton is the one, grab her.''

"It isn't that simple.''

"Life never is.''

"How many weddings have you planned for this month?'' he asked to distract her.

For the rest of the meal, they spoke of their work, then the unusual heat from a Santa Ana wind blowing in from the south. The humidity was about ten percent, and the trees planted along the streets had a tired, droopy appearance.

Just the way he felt, Cade reflected as he saw Emily to her car and headed for his office. A block down the street, he slowed his step. His father entered a store a couple of doors down. Cade approached the window and looked inside.

He saw Walter open a postal box and remove some mail. Most of it he tossed in a trash can. One letter he opened, read, then stuck in his jacket pocket.

For some reason, when his father exited, Cade turned to a coin-operated newspaper bin and pretended to read the headlines. After Walter proceeded down the street, clearly not returning to his office, Cade fell into step behind him.

To his surprise, Walter met a man Cade recognized—a bounty hunter who usually worked for bail bond firms to trace those who skipped out on their bail. Although the bounty hunters had some leeway under the law, this particular one was known to frequently stretch those boundaries.

The man handed Walter a small bag. Walter pulled a tape cassette from it, nodded to something the man said, then retraced his steps. Cade just managed to duck inside a dry-cleaning establishment before he was spotted. After making sure his father was past the place, he again followed.

This time Walter returned to his office over the jewelry store, which was two buildings up from the postal service place. Questions buzzed through Cade's head. His father was keeping unusual company these days, and he wondered why.

The private life of Walter Parks might prove interesting, he mused. Recalling he had an appointment to plan an estate trust, he hurried to his own office.

Sara vacuumed up her late dinner—a bowl of cereal she'd spilled all over the kitchen floor—then decided to vacuum the rest of the first-floor rooms since she'd done that only once since arriving in town.

Pushing the vacuum cleaner back and forth over the Oriental carpet in the elegant living room, she found it hard to believe that she'd arrived in San Francisco on Wednesday, exactly four weeks ago that day.

During that time, a person could move a thousand miles from home, teach two weeks, get fired, take a part-time job, investigate a murder and stupidly fall in love with the wrong person—all in twenty-eight days.

She summoned the anger that had carried her through the long winter. Love, she'd decided, was a trap for the unwary, especially for women. She wouldn't—

Her furious thoughts were interrupted by a noise at the back of the duplex. She flicked off the vacuum cleaner and listened. Hmm, must have been her imagination.

Just as she started to continue with the cleaning, she heard another knocking sound on the back door. She'd deliberately kept the door closed and the blinds drawn that week in order to avoid Stacy and her father. Since it was late, she knew it could only be one person.

Summoning anger around her like a cloak, she went to the den and opened the door. Cade, as she'd expected, stood there. "What is it?" she asked, keeping her voice neutral.

"I need to check on something," he said, sweeping by her before she could protest.

"What?" This time the question was belligerent. She didn't appreciate his high-handed ways. Besides, she had nothing to say to him. Nothing good, at any rate.

"I want to check your phone."

Without a by-your-leave, he unplugged the phone from the wall jack, lifted the receiver and unscrewed the ends.

"Why?" she demanded, moving closer so she could see exactly what he was up to.

"In case it's bugged."

She opened her mouth, then closed it. Since someone had tapped his father's phone, maybe the senior Parks had decided to reciprocate. Sitting on the coffee table, she peered at the phone parts in Cade's hands. "Do you see anything?"

He gave her a sardonic glance. "Yeah, but I wouldn't recognize a bug if it spit in my eye."

Meeting his candid gaze, she couldn't help but smile. He grinned at her. Her smile widened.

So they sat there, their knees almost touching, their heads only inches apart, and smiled at each other until she recalled she was angry. She changed her smile to the proper serious frown.

"Who would bug my phone?" she asked. "Walter Parks," she answered the question, then peered at the son to see how he took this accusation.

He nodded, his handsome face solemn as he studied her.

"I'll call Tyler." She retrieved the cell phone from her purse, called her brother and told him of Cade's suspicions.

"Be right there," her brother said. "I'll call Nick."

"Right. And thanks." She replaced the phone in her purse and returned to the den. "He'll be over soon."

Cade nodded while putting the receiver together. He plugged in the phone again, checked the dial tone, hung up, then settled back on the sofa.

Sara took a chair, and there they sat in total silence.

"Stacy misses you," he said after an eon had passed. "Don't hurt her because of the situation between us."

"I wouldn't," she protested. "I've been busy the last two days—"

"I've missed you, too," he interrupted.

She stared at him, then shrugged. "Sounds like a personal problem to me."

"You're stubborn, young Sara," he murmured. "I didn't remember that about you."

Crossing her arms as a barrier between them, she sat and glared at the wall behind him and refused to meet his gaze, which moved from one point to another as he continued his perusal of her.

When he focused on her mouth, hot tingles ran over her lips. When his gaze dropped lower, electric currents dashed helter-skelter through her body. If he didn't stop looking at her, she was going to explode—

The ring of the doorbell was a relief.

She sprinted down the hall and welcomed her brother and Nick Banning. "Hi, Nick. Oh, and Mark, too."

The three men entered and followed her to the den. "You think Sara's place is bugged?" Tyler asked.

"I think it's a good idea to check it out," Cade said.

"Why?"

Sara noticed her brother sounded as belligerent as she had earlier. She waited for Cade's answer.

"I saw my father with someone today." Cade glanced at Mark Banning when he mentioned the name and circumstances.

"I know him," Mark said. He stood. "I'll get to work."

"Let him do it," Nick advised when Tyler stood. "He knows the latest devices better than we do."

In the manner of a TV detective, Mark pulled on latex gloves, then removed a flashlight from his jacket pocket and went outside after a quick check inside. Fifteen minutes ticked by. Sara prepared iced tea and brought the glasses into the den on a tray.

When he returned, he looked pleased. "Bingo," he said and laid a tiny electronic snooping device on the coffee table. He stripped off the latex gloves and returned them to his pocket. "That was on Sara's line." He laid an identical one beside the other and looked at Cade. "This was on yours."

Sara's gaze flew to Cade.

He didn't look surprised as he gave her a slight smile before speaking to Mark. "Good work."

"How did you know?" Tyler asked.

"A hunch," Cade said. "If my father thought you

guys had tapped his telephone, it followed that he would return the favor. I didn't expect a second one, though.''

"So what do we do now?" Tyler gestured to the bugs.

"I'll take them." Cade reached for the devices, then looked at Mark. "Do I need to worry about fingerprints?"

"Probably not. The person who installed them is a pro. I don't imagine he was careless."

Cade nodded. "You got a plastic bag I can use?" he asked Sara.

She got one from the kitchen. They all observed as Cade securely closed the bag, with the transmitters inside, and put it in his pocket. He lifted his iced tea glass in a mock toast. "To the three musketeers and D'Artagnan." He glanced at the other three men, then at Sara.

"All for one and one for all," Tyler intoned and held his glass over the coffee table.

Sara, Tyler, Nick and Mark clinked glasses. She noticed that Cade hadn't joined them.

"Four musketeers," Tyler said, picking up on her thought.

"I'm just the messenger," Cade told them. "Or the traitor, according to which side one is on."

Mark checked his watch. "I have to be in court early in the morning. A guy was embezzling from the family business. His wife got suspicious about some invoices. Turns out they were from bogus companies.''

Sara saw her brother and their friends out. The den was empty when she returned. She turned off the lamps, leaving a night-light on, then went out on the deck.

Cade was there, a hip propped on the rail as he gazed at the cityscape.

"You're going to confront your father about the wiretapping,'' she said.

"Yes.''

"Is that wise?''

He shrugged.

"Maybe he didn't have anything to do with it.''

"Then he can deny any knowledge of it.''

"But you think he arranged it,'' she persisted.

"Yes.''

She hesitated, then said, "Cade, this isn't your fight. Don't alienate your family because of…'' She couldn't decide how to say it.

"Because of us, Sara?'' He turned so they faced each other. "Because of what you and I have shared? We've slept together. What does that mean nowadays?''

The cynical tone lashed her heart. "I wish we hadn't come here,'' she said in a low voice. "Maybe my mother was wrong about what occurred. Maybe your father told the truth and my father's death was one of those freak accidents that happen to people.''

He studied her for a long moment before replying.

"Maybe. Or maybe it wasn't. At any rate, twenty-five years is long enough to wonder about it. Whatever the truth, it's time it surfaced. Then and only then can the past be laid to rest." He turned back to viewing the night.

Sara wanted to go to him, but she couldn't. His manner was too closed, too remote. She didn't blame him for wanting nothing more to do with her. If they proved his father guilty of murder, it would be a serious blow to his family.

There seemed to be nothing more to discuss. She went inside and climbed the stairs to her bedroom. A simple wall divided the two town houses, but it may as well have been a thousand-mile rift.

Cade stood at the window of his office well before nine o'clock the next morning. He had the place to himself since the secretaries, clerks and law associates wouldn't be in until nine and most of the senior partners didn't arrive until ten o'clock or later.

It was a time for thinking, but his mind was curiously blank. He'd left word at his father's office that he wanted a meeting and would be there at noon. Too bad his morning was filled with appointments. He wanted this day behind him.

He heard Steve in the next office. He needed to talk to him, too. He went next door. "Hey," he said.

Steve hung his suit coat on a rack. "Good morning. You're in early." He picked up a container of coffee and blew across the surface before taking a sip.

Cade leaned against the door frame. "Yeah. I've been thinking about your proposition."

"And?"

"Let's go for it."

Steve looked comically surprised. "Damn, you mean it? You really will do it?"

Cade nodded and returned his friend's grin. "How soon can we move on it?"

Steve clicked on his computer. "I'm printing out my resignation right now."

"You've written it?" Cade asked.

"Yeah. You want a copy?"

Cade shook his head. "I'll manage. What date are you making it effective?"

"The end of August. That'll give me time to wrap up most of the crap, uh, I mean cases, that I have. What about you?"

"I'll use the same. Have you spoken to Mark Banning?"

"Not yet. Let's set up a lunch date, no, better make it dinner. This may take some planning."

"Okay, then."

Steve rose and held out his hand. "We may starve, but we'll do it on our own."

Cade nodded and shook his new partner's hand. A few hours later, he left the law firm and walked to his father's place of business. It was a day for change, he thought, going inside and up the stairs to the second floor.

The secretary's office was empty. She'd probably gone to lunch. Cade tapped on his father's door.

"Come in," Walter said.

He was smiling when Cade entered. Cade crossed the expensive carpet and stopped before his father's desk. He removed the plastic bag from his pocket and shook the contents out on the leather pad that protected the wood surface. "Let's compare transmitters," he said. "Are either of these like the one you said you found on your phone?"

He observed the mask that slid over his father's face and the fact that his eyes darted to the wall of cabinets that housed a television and other electronic gear.

"Where did you get these?" Walter asked.

"Sara's home line. And mine." Cade crossed to the built-in cabinets and opened a door. Upon checking, he found a tape cassette in the player. He hit the play button.

Sara's voice wafted into the room. She was talking to her friend, Rachel. The discussion was innocuous, girl talk about shopping, complaints about the school where Rachel still taught and plans to meet at lunch on Friday.

Cade turned the machine off when the women said goodbye. He removed the cassette and put it in the plastic bag. "Illegal wiretapping," Cade murmured, counting up the charges that would ensue if his father was caught. "Invasion of privacy. Conspiracy—"

"Conspiracy to do what?" Walter snapped.

"To prevent the truth from coming out about what happened to Jeremy Carlton?" Cade returned to the front of the desk. He met his father's glare. "Why, exactly, did you feel it necessary to bug my line, too?"

Walter's lip curled in a sneer. "You've lost your head over the girl, that's why. I needed to know what you were saying to her. You had a meeting at her place with her brother and his friends last week."

"We had another one last night. That's when Mark found the transmitters on our phone lines."

Cade noted the hardening of his father's features, the harshness of his expression and the coldly calculating gleam in his eyes. He wondered if, thirty years from now, he would look the same. He hoped not.

When Walter reached for the two transmitters, Cade scooped them up and replaced them in the bag, then stored the evidence in his pocket. "I'll keep these in a safe place," he said.

"You're getting a little too big for your britches, boy," Walter told him, his manner now threatening. "That can have serious consequences."

"Such as?" Cade challenged. "You'll get me fired? Too late. I turned in my resignation before I came over here."

Walter exploded. "You young fool, you don't know what you're doing. Or who you're dealing with. I can see that you don't get another job in this city."

Cade watched the pulse pound in his father's temple for a couple of seconds before answering. "And I can see that you don't do business with any reputable company in the state in the future. I know how to play that game. I've seen you do it often enough over the years when you wanted to get rid of a competitor."

"That was business," his father defended his actions.

"Yeah, but this is a felony." Cade patted his pocket. "I saw you with the bounty hunter. Lie down with dogs and you get up with fleas. Isn't that the way the saying goes?"

"Get out," Walter snarled. "You're no son of mine. I'm writing you out of my will. I never thought I would see the day when you, of all my children, would betray the family."

Cade thought of his mother, of his missing brother, of Sara and her family. "No," he said. "I guess you didn't."

He headed for the door.

"Just a minute," Walter said in a different tone. "We need to talk this over. Let's not go off half-cocked."

Cade shook his head and kept walking, out of the office, out of the building. He'd canceled his afternoon appointments, so he was free for the day. On the street, he walked aimlessly until he stood at Pier 39, crowded with tourists and street mimes, shops and restaurants.

A lot of the things he'd done in his life had been

for his father's approval, Cade realized. Good grades, a position with a prestigious law firm, marriage to the daughter of a prominent family. Children wanted to please the most important people in their world.

An utter weariness seeped into his soul. He and Em had known the happier days in their family's history. They'd tried to uphold the illusion that that family still existed.

Rowan and Jessica had never been fooled into thinking all was well in their household. At nearly thirty, it was time he, too, recognized their father for the ruthless, ambitious man he was, one who would destroy others who got in the way of his plans.

Murder?

Cade didn't know about that. He was getting off the merry-go-round of his father's schemes for his own reasons. He and Stacy were going to have a life separate and different from the usual Parks family strife.

His daughter had good instincts when it came to people. Stacy had never been comfortable around her grandfather. While he wouldn't deny all contact, he would see to it that his child wasn't subjected to Walter's vitriol or verbal attacks on the people he didn't like. Otherwise, he would make it clear there would be no visits at all.

At last his anger ebbed. Noting it was nearly three o'clock, he returned to his car and drove home. Tai and Stacy were surprised by his appearance. He told

Tai she could take the rest of the day off. He and Stacy were going to the zoo.

"Let's go," Stacy said enthusiastically after she'd put on shoes and washed her face and hands. When they were on their way, she sighed loudly.

"What?" he asked.

"I wish Sara could go with us," she said. "The zoo is her abs'lutely favorite thing."

His insides clenched as if preparing for a sucker punch to the gut. "She's at work."

"I know, but it would be nice if she could be with us, wouldn't it?"

"Yeah," he said. "It would be nice."

That was the one thing he hadn't faced yet—his feelings about Sara. What was real between them, and what was simply her using him and Stacy for her own ends? Were she and his father two of a kind?

Good question, he admitted with a cynicism that was new to him. Too bad there wasn't an answer.

Chapter Thirteen

Sara set up her easel on the deck Saturday morning and began sketching the view of the ocean from there. After seeing Cade and Stacy leave, probably for the ranch, she'd decided to do a watercolor of the scene. Anything to keep busy so she wouldn't have to think.

Yesterday the principal at Lakeside had called and asked her to return to her teaching post. Since it was the one thing she loved without reservation, she decided it was foolish to let pride prevent her from continuing her chosen profession. She'd told Mrs. Ling later that afternoon.

The ice-cream shop owner had approved the decision wholeheartedly. She informed Sara that her grandson missed Miss Carlton and wanted her back as his teacher.

It was nice to be wanted, Sara mused, putting a bright face on the situation. The false cheer lasted but a moment, then she was in the doldrums again.

She missed Cade and his daughter. She wanted to go to the ranch with them. She also wanted to show the world what Walter Parks had done to her father. She couldn't have it both ways. They were mutually exclusive actions.

Choices. Did she have any?

Not really. Her loyalty lay with her family just as Cade's belonged to his. This path, the one seeking justice, had been chosen when she and Tyler had decided to leave Denver and come to San Francisco. She couldn't hate Walter Parks and love the son. It didn't make sense.

A sigh escaped her. She was angry with herself, with Cade and with the fate that had put her in this position.

When was life going to smooth out and be easy for the children of Marla Carlton?

"Yoo-hoo," a voice called from the side of the mansion.

Sara recognized Rachel's voice and went to open the gate. "Come in. I'm glad to see you. I need a distraction from my own thoughts, which are driving me insane."

"I rang the doorbell but got no answer. Since your car was here, I wasn't sure if you were being reclusive or were out on the deck," Rachel told her. "Oh, you're painting. I've never seen any of your stuff. That's very good."

Her friend stood on the deck and gazed at the drawing, then at the scene it depicted.

"Thanks," Sara said. "I needed something to do today."

Rachel studied her. "I understand you're coming back to school and your job there."

"Yes. Cade got it straightened out."

"How?"

Sara told her as much as she knew.

"He must have put it rather strongly to his father," Rachel said. Her eyes narrowed as she gazed at Sara.

"What?" Sara demanded, brushing a pale blue wash on the sky portion of the canvas.

"I think he must care for you a lot."

"I think he convinced his father that putting a bug on my phone line wasn't the wisest thing to do."

Rachel's eyes went wide. "Are you kidding?"

"I wish," Sara said. "First, Cade accused me and Tyler of doing the same to his father's telephone, then he decided his father may have reciprocated. Mark Banning found the transmitters on my line...and on Cade's."

"His father listened in on Cade's conversations?" Rachel was astounded. "What is going on in that family?"

Sara swished the brush in a glass of water, wiped it on a towel and stuck it in another glass, bristles up to dry. "I don't know. Cade and I haven't spoken in a couple of days."

"Is it all off between you two?"

Sara shrugged. "When was it ever on?" she asked

sardonically. "I was a fool to get mixed up with him."

Rachel nodded. "It's hard, but you get over it."

Sara wondered if her friend was thinking of her former husband and his behavior, bringing her to a strange city, then leaving one day without a word. Luckily Rachel had her teaching credentials and the job at Lakeside.

Life went on.

Putting on a cheerful front, Sara spent the rest of the day with the other teacher. Rachel told her all the gossip from school and Sara related all that had happened on the search for the missing uncle.

"So far, no luck," she finished the tale. "But I have great faith in Mark after seeing him in action when he found the transmitters."

"Until your investigation is finished, there's not much hope for you and Cade, is there?"

Sara didn't speak for a second, then she said, "There's no hope at all." She even managed a smile.

Cade hit the garage door opener, then pulled into the narrow space and cut off the engine. He'd planned to stay at the ranch until the next day as usual, but a restlessness he couldn't control had seized him after dinner that evening and wouldn't let go.

Stacy had fallen asleep while watching her favorite video. He'd decided to return to town. She was now asleep in the child safety seat behind him. He unbuckled and climbed out, then carried his daughter up to her bedroom.

After changing her into pajamas over her objections, he put her to bed and started to leave. "Wait, Daddy," Stacy said, then gave a big yawn. "I haven't said my prayers."

He recognized the delaying tactic for what it was. Schooling himself to patience, he sat on the side of the bed. "Okay, I'm listening."

She went through the usual list of "God bless Daddy and Mary Blue-eyes and Grandpa Parks and Grandpa and Grandma Limbini and Aunt Emily and Aunt Jessica and Uncle Rowan—"

"Wrap it up," he murmured.

She nodded and spoke faster. "And Wheelie and Sara," she finished.

He started to rise.

"And please, God, give me and my daddy a fam'bly—"

"Family," he corrected, frowning as the prayer grew unexpectedly longer.

"A fam'ly that plays and has fun like we did with Sara and Teddy and Rufus at the lighthouse and beach, and a baby brother we can teach to ride like we did Sara, and we'll all be nice and always do the right thing because we love each other. And please, please make Sara like us again. Amen."

Cade felt as if he'd been hit with a sledgehammer as the prayer ended and Stacy turned over on her back so he could rub her.

"Are you going to rub my back?" she asked when he didn't move.

"Yes," he managed to say past the mangled lump

of pain and longing and a lot of other emotions that had gathered in his throat.

After tucking the sheet around her shoulders, he rubbed up and down her back in gentle strokes. His daughter seemed suddenly tiny and fragile to him. She was still a very young child with a child's dreams and hopes.

Stacy had never complained to him about a lack of family. She'd never cried because she didn't have a mother like the other kids in her class. She seemed happy and confident, so he'd thought having him and Tai was enough.

He'd thought wrong.

The quiet earnestness in her voice during the prayer caused an ache inside him that he couldn't explain. Her request for a baby brother had touched him deeply, as had her promise that they would all be nice and love one another.

He wondered how much she remembered of the quarrels between him and her mother, how much she knew of the tension between him and her grandfather.

"Ah, Stace," he said on a low groan of sorrow.

His child had never had the loving home she'd prayed for. Neither had he, not after his mother had been sent away. He realized he still missed her. Her laughter. Her gentleness and kindness, her kisses when he'd scraped his knees. Stacy had missed those things, too.

He'd provided them as best he could, but it hadn't been enough. That was evident by the request to have Sara in their lives once more. Sara had supplied the one thing he couldn't—a woman's touch. A girl needed a woman as a role model as much as a boy needed a father to teach him to be an honorable man.

A family. Another child. Love. Sara.

The words flowed over him, through him. He closed his eyes as light dawned inside him, as warm and real as the rising of the sun. He and Stacy wanted the same things, and he could give them to her...and to any other children he might have, that Sara might give him.

Sara.

All he had to do was convince her to marry the son of her family's sworn enemy. Could any marriage work based on that premise? It was a chance he was willing to take.

After he was sure Stacy was asleep, Cade quietly left the room, went downstairs and out on the deck. A night-light was on in the den at Sara's place, but she wasn't visible in the room.

He couldn't recall if her car had been in its usual spot. Was she out for the evening? Or was she gone for good?

A jolt of fear went right down his spine and lodged in the innermost part of his body. If she'd left, he could find her. He knew where her brother worked.

At that moment, the foyer light came on in her side of the house as she entered the front door. He saw her lock the dead bolt, place her purse on the hall table, flick the light off, then come toward him.

She stopped in the kitchen. When she appeared again, she carried a cup and was dunking a tea bag up and down in it as she settled on the sofa, then kicked off her shoes.

Emotion erupted in his chest. Joy, relief and apprehension jostled for position. Taking a calming breath, he knocked on her door and tried to compose an opening line that would make sense.

Sara was startled at the tap on the back door and sloshed a few drops of hot tea on her jeans. She and Rachel had been out to dinner, then had taken in a movie of murder and dark deeds in a small town where everyone thought they knew everyone else. They'd been in for a shock.

Which was the way she felt as she rose and unlocked the door. She cleared her throat and ordered her heart to slow down and beat steadily. "Yes?"

"May I come in?"

"Why?" she asked, unable to think of a thing they needed to talk about.

His smile did things to her insides. "Because," he said.

He gazed into her eyes with an expression she couldn't read, but it confused her nevertheless. She moved aside.

When he entered, the room seemed to fill with life and energy and music…yes, music, although she couldn't tell where it came from. She closed the door against the cool breeze that flowed inside.

Gesturing toward one of the chairs, she resumed her position on the sofa and tucked her feet under her. "Would you like a cup of tea?" she asked politely.

He shook his head and sat on the sofa, then placed

a monitor on the coffee table so they could hear Stacy in case she awoke. "Sara," he said, then was silent.

"Yes?" His stare was making her so nervous she was afraid she might drop the cup. She realized she had to take charge of the situation, or else she might melt into a puddle on the carpet. "Yes?" she said more strongly.

Cade didn't blame her for watching him warily. He wanted to dispense with explanations and take her into his arms. He wanted to kiss her until neither of them could breathe. "Tonight I had a life-changing experience."

The delicate arch of her eyebrows rose in question when he paused and smiled at the dramatic opening. The beautiful green eyes didn't waver from his face as she waited for him to continue. No smile appeared on her alluring mouth.

"I listened to my daughter say her prayers," he continued, solemn again. "She asked for a family, a baby brother and our friend Sara to like us again."

He saw the soft pink lips tremble slightly. He observed as she raised the cup and took a sip, hiding behind its steamy surface until she had her emotions under control. He knew this woman. He knew her well.

"I've never stopped liking Stacy," she said. "I'll make a point of telling her tomorrow, also that I'm returning to the classroom Monday. I've decided to resume teaching. Although working in the ice-cream shop has been fun," she added as if worried he might think she hadn't liked it.

"Good." It felt like a step in the right direction, but there was more he had to say. "I realized tonight that I wanted the same things as my five-year-old daughter—a family, perhaps more children…and for my friend Sara to like me again."

Sara was completely taken by surprise. "I—I—well, of course I like you. That is…" She faded into silence.

"What I really want," he continued, "is for you to love me. As I love you. I want to give Stacy that little brother she mentioned, but only if you're the other part of the package. I want us to be a family."

She started shaking her head before he finished.

"Why not?" he demanded, but gently.

"It wouldn't work, Cade. Even if my mother was wrong, I could never like your father. I don't think I could stand being in his house. It would be a constant source of discord between us, and it wouldn't be fair to Stacy or the children we might have. You'll have to find someone else."

She clasped the cup tightly as she delivered this last bit of hurtful advice. Heaven help her, she did love him, but a life with him was impossible. Impossible!

"I've severed ties with my father."

While she digested this, he removed the cup from her hands and set it aside, then he moved closer so she felt his presence as warmth that permeated her whole being. She'd missed him, she realized.

"I've missed you," he said.

For a second, she was afraid she'd said the words aloud. "Please, don't."

"Don't miss you? I can't help it. Don't love you? I can't stop. I don't want to, not ever."

She put her hands over her eyes. They felt hot and achy as pressure built behind them. "It wouldn't work."

"Why not, Sara? If we work really, really hard at it, I think we can do it. A friend and I are going to open our own law office, so there'll be a lot of changes in our lives," he murmured. "We can handle it. I have great faith in you and Stacy. You two will know how to head off problems."

A thousand fragments of scattered thoughts roiled around in Sara's brain. She couldn't make them settle into any order at all. "Cade…"

"Yes?"

He leaned closer, crowding her into the corner, then he cupped her face and kissed her tenderly.

"I can't breathe when you do that," she whispered as he continued to kiss each corner of her mouth, then her eyes, her temple, ear, throat, chin, and back to her lips.

"Marry me, Sara. Make all my dreams come true."

His voice was the south wind, warm and fragrant with the promise of flowers and spring buds, of life and growing things…babies…

"How can we?" she asked. "Your father—"

"My loyalty is to my wife," he told her, lifting his head and looking earnestly into her eyes. "Trust me, Sara. That's the one thing I have to have from you.

Besides your love. Give me those, and I'll give you everything that a man can give to the woman he loves. That's my pledge to you.''

She didn't know whether to laugh or cry, so she did a bit of both. He kissed the few tears that spilled over her lashes and pulled her into his arms by the simple expedient of lifting her slender body into his lap.

"Sara, Sara," he said in a low, heartfelt growl, "I've waited for years for you to come back to me. Don't leave me now."

In the battle between love and war that raged inside her, the outcome was assured. Love won.

She wrapped her arms around his neck and pressed her face into his throat. She smelled the intoxicating aroma of his soap and talc and skin, the essence that was his alone, and knew she couldn't deny her heart its hunger for a home.

"I can't," she said.

"Can't love me?" he asked, his eyes dark as he gazed into her eyes.

She shook her head. "I can't leave you. I love you, too." She smoothed her hands over his lean cheeks and gazed her fill of his beloved face. "You always lived in my heart. You were my first love. My only love."

He stopped breathing for a few seconds, then exhaled in relief as her words penetrated all the way to the center of his soul. "As you are mine, young Sara."

They kissed for long, slow, mind-dazzling minutes,

then snuggled together on the comfortable sofa, hunger growing as they gave free rein to their feelings.

Cade fitted his body carefully over hers, their arms and legs entwined like the strongest love vine. "When can we be married?" he asked. "I don't want to wait."

"I don't, either," she admitted.

"Next weekend we could drive to Tahoe and be married on the Nevada side. I want some time alone with you. Em won't mind having Stacy—"

"No, Stacy should be with us. She'll want to take part," Sara told him. "Or plan the whole ceremony."

They smiled at each other in understanding.

"I know. Your twin sister can be your best woman and my brother can be my man of honor. After the wedding lunch, they can bring Stace back with them and we can have a night to ourselves for a honeymoon."

His grin was wicked. "A one-night stand for a honeymoon, huh? I like the sounds of that."

Sara poked him in the ribs, then kissed him in mad delight until they both went a little crazy. "I came here seeking vengeance. I found something wonderful." She laid a hand in the middle of his chest. "You. Your love. It's like getting a gift for being alive, a reward for surviving. How does one give thanks for such bounty?"

"By sticking it out together," he said, laying his hand over hers. "By being the parents our children need. By loving each other all our lives."

She took a deep breath. "My word of honor," she said.

"And mine."

They sealed it with a kiss.

"So when is Stacy going to get that baby brother she wants?" Sara asked. "She told me last week she thought it was time. Her best friend has two little brothers. She feels she's getting behind."

Cade laughed. Sara loved the carefree sound of it and the happiness that inspired it. He nuzzled her ear.

"We can start right away," he suggested in the sexiest voice.

"A man after my own heart." Closing her eyes as they melded together, she realized she had found the one eternal truth—home *is* where the heart is.

Hers was here, in the arms of her beloved.

*   *   *   *   *

Don't miss the next book in
THE PARKS EMPIRE
DIAMONDS AND DECEPTIONS
by Marie Ferrarella
Silhouette Special Edition #1627

Find out what happens when Private Investigator Mark Banning finds the Carltons' long-lost uncle—and his beautiful daughter!

Available August 2004
wherever Silhouette Books are sold

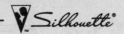

SPECIAL EDITION™

A sweeping new family saga

THE PARKS EMPIRE

Dark secrets. Old lies. New loves.

Twenty-five years ago, Walter Parks got away with murder…or so he thought. But now his children have discovered the truth, and they will do anything to clear the family name—even if it means falling for the enemy!

Don't miss these books from six favorite authors:

ROMANCING THE ENEMY
by Laurie Paige
(Silhouette Special Edition #1621, on sale July 2004)

DIAMONDS AND DECEPTIONS
by Marie Ferrarella
(Silhouette Special Edition #1627, on sale August 2004)

THE RICH MAN'S SON by Judy Duarte
(Silhouette Special Edition #1634, on sale September 2004)

THE PRINCE'S BRIDE by Lois Faye Dyer
(Silhouette Special Edition #1640, on sale October 2004)

THE MARRIAGE ACT by Elissa Ambrose
(Silhouette Special Edition #1646, on sale November 2004)

THE HOMECOMING by Gina Wilkins
(Silhouette Special Edition #1652, on sale December 2004)

Available at your favorite retail outlet.

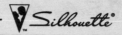

SPECIAL EDITION™

From award-winning author
MARIE FERRARELLA

Diamonds and Deceptions
(Silhouette Special Edition #1627)

When embittered private investigator
Mark Banning came to San Francisco in
search of a crucial witness, he didn't expect
to fall in love with beautiful bookworm
Brooke Moss—daughter of the very man he
was searching for. Mark did everything in his
power to keep Brooke out of his investigation,
but ultimately had to face the truth—he couldn't
do his job without breaking her heart....

DARK SECRETS.
OLD LIES.
NEW LOVES.

Available at your favorite retail outlet.

HARLEQUIN®
flipside

It's all about me!

Coming in July 2004,

Harlequin Flipside heroines tell you exactly what they think...in their own words!

WHEN SIZE MATTERS
by Carly Laine
Harlequin Flipside #19

WHAT PHOEBE WANTS
by Cindi Myers
Harlequin Flipside #20

I promise these first-person tales will speak to you!

**Look for Harlequin Flipside
at your favorite retail outlet.**

COMING NEXT MONTH